COMBAT CORPSMAN

The Al Anbar Chronicles: First Marine Expeditionary Force—Iraq

Book 2

Col Jonathan P. Brazee, USMCR (Ret)

Semper Fi Press

A Semper Fi Press Book

August 2013

Copyright © 2013 by Jonathan Brazee

ISBN-13: 978-0615867977 (Semper Fi Press)
ISBN-10: 0615867979

Printed in the United States of America

This is a work of fiction. All of the characters, names, and dialogue in this novel are either the products of the author's imagination or are used fictitiously. Some on the incidents used in this book are based on actual events; however, the details, timing, and units involved have been changed. The units described in the book were real units deployed to Iraq during the time frame, but the personnel and events described are fictitious.

Acknowledgements:
I want to thank all those who took the time to pre-read this book, catching my mistakes in both content and typing. From VFW Post 9951 in Bangkok, I need to thank MacAlan Thompson for his proofreading and fact-checking. I need to thank my editor, Jenn Scranton, for her excellent work. And most of all, from military.com, I need to thank a real combat corpsman, HMCS Ron Martin. His help was invaluable in making this book as accurate as possible. Any remaining typos and inaccuracies are solely my fault.

This book is dedicated to all US Navy Corpsman who have served with their brothers in arms in the US Marine Corps.

Prologue

HM A "Corps" School, Naval School of Health Sciences, Balboa Naval Medical Center, San Diego

"So, Zach, you ready to get your golden ticket?"

I turned around to see Devon Harris coming up to me from behind, a broad smile on his face. Devon was the class honor graduate, a position I had hoped to earn, but his enthusiasm was so infectious that it was hard to be jealous of him.

"Yea, Balboa, here I come!"

"You deserve it, bro. Come on, let's get in and make it official," he said, clapping a hand on my shoulder.

This was the culmination of a lot of planning; but still, I felt a degree of nervous excitement. It had only been year ago that I had gone up the steps to get my high school diploma, looking forward to whatever my future had to bring. I had no idea that the path to my future had already been mapped out. Unbeknownst to either of us at the time, Amy was already pregnant with Tyson, gotten that way on prom night. Yea, on prom night. Pretty cliché, huh?

We found out Amy was pregnant at the end of June, and after a quick trip to the county administration center down on Pacific Avenue, we were married. It may not have been the wedding Amy had wanted, but we had been going together for two years and I think both of us knew we would end up together even if we had never actually made the announcement.

My mom was happy. She liked Amy, and with us getting hitched at the county, she didn't have to come up with the money for a wedding. Amy's parents sure wouldn't have been able to help out. They spent pretty much every penny over at Barona Casino and never paid too much attention to their youngest daughter.

We moved into a crappy apartment in El Cajon, but at $500 per month, it wasn't that bad. What was bad was trying to find a job, one that paid the bills and offered medical. With Amy getting rounder, we needed coverage.

I took some odd jobs, but what I really wanted to do was to be a medical technician. I saw an ad on TV about getting trained as a radiology tech, and when I researched it online, it seemed that jobs in the medical field were going to be in huge demand in the future. The only problem was that the training cost money and took up to two years. Amy was going to pop long before that.

It was then that my brother told me to join the Army. He had enlisted and even been in on the invasion of Iraq. He got out after his enlistment was up, and he regretted it. I didn't want to go to Iraq, though. I was a homeboy, not a warrior. And I wanted to be in San Diego for my baby's birth. So I went to the Navy recruiter. He guaranteed me the HM field and told me I could go to C School after becoming a basic corpsmen so I could get trained in a specialty field. I could even serve right at Balboa Naval Medical Center, not even ten miles from our apartment.

Amy had been afraid that I would go off to war, but after assuring her I would stay in San Diego, she gave her blessing. I had gone to Great Lakes for boot, then came back to San Diego for Corps School just as Tyson was born. Today, we were getting told our assignments. Everyone else knew what I wanted; I sure told anyone who would lend me an ear my plans. Radiology was my first choice as I could easily get a job at Sharp or Kaiser Permanente after my enlistment was up, but really, any hospital training would do. If I had been the honor graduate, I would have been guaranteed my next billet, but from what my recruiter had told me before I signed up, I really wasn't worried.

We took our seats in the classroom. We still had follow-on training to do, but this was the day when our Navy service would really sink in. This was when we would be told what we would be doing and where. I had talked to the chief about my assignment, and I was pretty sure I was staying in San Diego, but this was the Navy and you never knew. I had done well in Corps School, so I should get my choice, but in reality, if there was a Navy hospital there, I could get stationed there.

I looked around the room. A good portion of the other students would be going to the Fleet Marine Force, or the FMF, as we call it, the poor saps. They might as well be Marines. Some of them, like Mike Pulante over there, actually enlisted for that. He could have it as far as I was concerned. I'll serve in a nice air conditioned, clean hospital, getting training for a long and profitable career after the Navy, thank you very much.

One of our instructors, HM1 Teller, walked up to the class podium, papers in hand. We immediately quieted down. He started telling us all about serving as a corpsman, how every billet was important, yada yada yada. I just wanted shout out for him to get going. At last, he looked down at the papers and begun to give the assignments.

"Aguilar, Reynaldo," he intoned, "The *USS Nimitz*, Naval Station Everett, Washington."

The first billet was a fleet billet. Rey wouldn't be going to C School, at least not on this tour. He would be shipboard and probably off on deployment before he knew what hit him.

The next few billets were either ships or the Marines. Josh Allen got the *Ronald Reagan* out of right here in San Diego. Anderson N. got the *USS Denver* in Sasebo, and Anderson S. got the Marines. Then Tricia Astor got Naval Clinic Hawaii, which raised a murmur. Hawaii was considered a plum billet. She would be in a clinic, but without a C school. No hospital billets had been assigned yet. It looked like I would be the first one.

Toby Battle got the Marines, and that caused a different kind of murmur. Despite his name, Toby was not the most impressive physical specimen, and he had been adamant that he would not serve with the Marines. He looked shell-shocked. Well, better him than me, I thought.

When John Byzewski got his billet, also the Marines. I knew I was up next. I leaned forward eagerly.

"Cannon, Zachary. Second Marine Division, via TEMDUINS Field Medical Service School, Camp Lejeune."

Chapter 1

Camp Fallujah, Iraq
Feb 28, 2006

The first Marine was rushed into the ER. He was filthy, covered with Iraqi sand. The scarlet staining his arm seemed too bright, too saturated for the rest of him. All of the docs, nurses and corpsmen rushed to him; two of the senior docs talking over each other, each trying to take charge.

This was our first casualty. We weren't all even in-country yet. II MEF was still on the scene, and I MEF was just beginning to come in. I had been at Fallujah for two days now, part of our advance party coming in from our final training in Kuwait, which was why I was at the hospital. With only a handful of Marines from the company here, there wasn't much for me to do, so HM2 Sylvester had sent me to the hospital to help out while manning was in flux.

The Marine was a LCpl Miller, and he had been shot in the arm while out on a routine orientation convoy. No one had expected any action, but this was a war zone, after all, and the enemy didn't usually play by our rules.

I had rushed to the ER when the word had passed about incoming casualties, but there was nothing for me to do. The place was packed with people trying to get involved, and I was just an untrained HA. Still, I got a good look at Miller, at his drawn face and the mangled arm. I didn't feel queasy, per se, but still, I didn't feel completely normal. It was one thing to go treat simulated casualties with moulages back at Corps School or at FMSS at Camp Johnson, but it was another thing to see bits of human bone coming out of the skin. I hoped when it was me out there trying to treat a Marine that I would be calm and professional.

I stepped aside as the second Marine was brought in. He was a corporal whose name I didn't quite catch. He was unconscious, but had no visible wounds. Some of the docs shifted over to him, so I sort of insinuated myself in that group. I didn't actually get involved with the physical examination, but I hovered, trying to look like I was contributing. I didn't want anyone to order me out of there for just being in the way. After his flak jacket and deuce gear had been taken off and dropped on the floor, I scurried forward and grabbed them, pulling them and out of the way.

One of the doctors, a captain, had taken charge of the Marine. He performed a complete medical assessment, announcing each step and his finding as he completed each one. The corpsman in the field had placed a collar on the corporal, and that was left in place. Finally, the doctor seemed satisfied. He ordered an MRI, and one of the nurses grabbed me to help push the surgical table to radiology.

I thought it was ironic that even if I didn't get C-School for radiology, my first real assignment as an HA was taking someone there.

For all the hustle and bustle in the ER, I was left alone with Cpl Xenakis, as his chart labeled him. I took him to radiology, then sat and waited until he was done. Then, it was to the ICU to wait for him to recover. A nurse checked him over and helped me shift him into one of the beds. Dr. Whipple, the captain who had done the initial assessment, and someone who was probably the radiologist came and discussed the results. It seemed like our corporal was lucky. The IED that had taken out his hummer had probably given him a slight concussion and banged him up a bit, and he had taken a round in the chest that his flak jacket had stopped, but he seemed not to be in too bad shape.

"OK, then, let's let him wake up, then I want a chest X-ray to make sure he doesn't have any broken ribs. You, what's your name?" asked the doctor.

"HA Cannon, sir," I told him.

I was probably supposed to be in my cammies here as I was just lending an extra hand, but I had grabbed a set of scrubs and put them on, and with no name tag nor rank insignia, I was pretty much incognito. With two sets of medical teams though, the incoming and the outgoing, no one really thought it odd that someone they didn't know was there.

"OK, Cannon, he's resting well now with good vitals. As long as those remain steady, just wait until he comes to, take him back to radiology for a chest X-ray, then get him cleaned up. I'm going to want him to stay overnight, at least, for observation."

Both docs and the nurse left, leaving me alone with the Marine. He was a big guy, pretty buff, but he looked vulnerable laying there on the bed. If such a big guy could be taken out like that, I wondered what would happen when it was my turn to go out there into the fray.

"Can I come in?" a voice called out.

I looked up to see a head sticking in the door. A dirty, disheveled head. I walked over and was surprised to see the cross of a chaplain on his collar.

"I was with the corporal, and I'd like to come in to see him," the chaplain told me, looking in to catch a glimpse of the corporal.

In back of him were a few staff NCOs, including a first sergeant. I knew Xenakis needed to rest, but how do you keep a chaplain out?

"OK, sir, you can go in, but please just sit there for now. Cpl Xenakis is fine, but we want him to remain quiet for now. The rest of you, I'll let you know when you can see him."

The first sergeant nodded respectfully. None of my petty officers or chiefs had given me much respect in training, and here a first sergeant, the same as a senior chief, was giving me, a mere HA, respect. I'd heard that the Marines valued their corpsmen, but this seemed a bit much. Not that I was complaining.

The chaplain and I went back to sit beside Xenakis, who was breathing easily. There was a bit of blood on one of the chaplain's fingers, and I took a look at it, trying to muster an attitude of competence. He had a small scratch on the finger, but I told him to have it checked with as much authority as I could inflect into my voice.

I had to use the head. An ICU was normally manned all the time when there was a patient there, but evidently, this was not considered serious, and LCpl Miller was still in surgery, so I was left here alone. But with the chaplain there, I thought I could slip out and take a piss.

As I came back, I saw that Xenakis was awake, talking to the chaplain.

"I see you're awake. You feeling OK now?" I asked.

"Not too good, to be honest," he told me.

I gave a rueful laugh.

"Yeah, I would imagine so. You're going to be pretty sore for a few days. None of that's too serious, but you've got a concussion, and we're going to keep you overnight for observation. If you're feeling up to it, let's get you cleaned up, and Doctor Whipple's ordered a chest x-ray, just to be on the safe side."

I turned to the chaplain and said, "You might as well get cleaned up, too, sir. I'll take care of Xenakis now."

He looked at me, obviously torn.

"You go, sir. Get cleaned up. When LCpl Miller's out of surgery, he might need you," the corporal told him.

That seemed to register, because he got up, wished the corporal well, and left, but not before promising to be back to check up on him.

"We kept your first sergeant and the rest out, but the chaplain, he insisted on staying until you woke up," I said, bringing a wheelchair up to the bed. "Well, let's get going."

"I don't need that thing," he started to protest.

"Sorry there, corporal. But you've taken a knock on the head, and regs are regs. You get yours truly as your personal chauffeur. And here, you might want more of this," I said.

I don't know if it really was regs as I wasn't trained in this, but it made sense to me, and I would rather be over-cautious than under. I handed him the tube of cream the nurse had left behind.

He took it, then looked at me questioningly.

"For your lips. You got burned there, where you weren't covered up. Your gear saved you from being burnt anywhere else. We kept your gear after we took it off you. Most of it can't be used anymore, but it might make a good souvenir."

With that, I pushed him out the hatch and down to radiology.

Chapter 2

Hurricane Point, Ramadi
March 16, 2006

I let out a loud burp, the taste of bacon coming back up.

"Shit, Doc, didn't your mama teach you better than that?" Cpl Deacon asked, pulling back in distaste.

"Like the immortal Shrek proclaimed, 'Better out than in, I always say.' "

"Yea, Shrek's a fucking ogre, too. Just keep that shit inside of you when we're out there. I don't want the entire Al Qaeda to know we're coming."

"Aye-aye, there Cpl Deacon, sir, yes sir!" I answered, coming to an exaggerated, knee flapping attention and British-style salute.

He merely snorted and went to look at his fire team. I was one of the junior, if not the most junior, member of the squad, yet I was given a good deal of leeway and more respect than a PFC, my equivalent rank in the Marines, might receive. I had heard all of this at Corps School and FMSS, but it wasn't until we were out here in the Sandbox that I began to understand it. I didn't want to serve with the FMF, and I would go back in a minute if they let me, but still, I had to admit that this was one aspect of serving with the Marines that I liked.

If I had to serve with the Marines, at least it could have been at the hospital back at Fallujah. I had helped out there for almost a week before the rest of the battalion came aboard and we moved down here to Hurricane Point at Ramadi.

At Fallujah, I had hung out with medical personnel, even the doctors. Doc Willis, for example, had taken me under his wing. He was a reservist, a gastroenterologist with a practice in Beverly Hills, an ass doctor to the stars, as he called himself. He had been recalled to active duty, and each day he was in Iraq cost him thousands in lost medical fees and in keeping his practice open. Having a willing ear was cathartic to him, I guess, and he offered me a place with this practice when we got back. I'm not so sure I would really want to be a colonoscopy cowboy, but the money he mentioned was way more than I would have guessed.

Fallujah was a much more comfortable place to live, too. The barracks were OK, but the chow was great. We had a 24 hour ice cream bar, burgers, steaks, even prime rib on the weekends. Here at Hurricane Point, well, we had hot chow, but the variety was limited and so the menu was already getting boring—and we had not even been here a week yet. Well, not everything was boring. We got daily mortar and rocket rounds hitting in the camp, but no one had been hit yet.

Fallujah was big, too, with lots and lots of Marines. At the Point, we had the battalion and a few others, but not much else.

And now, we were leaving even that bit of security. My platoon was going on a short patrol around the camp. We know the camp had been under surveillance, and we had taken some sniper rounds among the indirect fire. The battalion CO thought that was messed up, that the insurgents could get to that close to camp, and he wanted us to keep active to keep the bad guys back from our perimeter. The National Guard, who had been in-country for almost a year, was still doing the major patrolling and combat ops out of Camp Ramadi and Camp Corregidor, but this was our backyard, and we had to secure it. This was going to be our third patrol. Nothing much happened on our first two, so I didn't expect much on this one. But still, I felt the butterflies. This was exactly why I didn't want to be with the FMF. I was weighed down with 60 or 70 pounds worth of gear, I was hot and tired just standing there, and I could have someone shooting at me soon. The radiology lab back at Balboa would be so much better a proposition.

We had up-armored hummers and even a few LAVs, so I wasn't sure why we were going out on foot. Ramadi was more suited for a MAP, the Mobile Assault Platoon, and we had been trained in that, but like the other two times, we were going like regular infantry. Sgt Butler, my squad leader, a guy on his third pump to the Sandbox, said it was just a show of force, to remind the bad guys that we were paying attention. If we were really going into the attack, we would be going full bore, ready for bear.

I didn't pay much attention to the op order. All I really had to do was follow Sgt Butler and render aid if anyone needed it. It wasn't like I was assigned to a fire team to kick ass and take names. I was armed, of course, but I wasn't sure that was even necessary. I didn't plan on shooting anyone. Yea, I know that corpsmen get right in the thick of things. At FMSS, we got a history class on all the corpsmen who received the Medal of Honor. Since WWI, all 18 of them had served with the Marines, and 12 had died earning the medal. Several had fought back, and one guy had killed a bunch of Japanese soldiers while saving his commander—at one point, holding an IV up with one hand and shooting a .45 with his other.

Jonathan P. Brazee

But I didn't expect that I would be doing any fighting. I was there to treat Marines, not be one.

When the order came to move out, we moved past the plywood SWAs that made up our buildings on the camp. I wasn't sure why we called them SWAs, and I sure didn't care for them as far as living conditions. They let in sand and hot air, then kept the heat in even after it started cooling down a bit. The Seabees had installed an air conditioner in each one, but they couldn't really keep up with the heat.

We trooped past the "Complacency Kills" sign someone had painted in red on a piece of plywood. The so-called front gate of the camp had more of the temporary look of the rest of the camp. Plywood and HESCO barriers were main theme running through the base, with green sandbags on the roofs thrown in for a bit of a fashion accent.

First squad went out first, followed by the platoon commander and his headquarters. We were Tail-End Charlie, behind Third. As we passed the front gate and made our way past the barriers, I couldn't help but feel a shiver run down my spine. We were not going far, just to check out two buildings less than 200 meters away, but still, we were in Indian country.

We moved slowly, but steadily. The sun was up in force, and with all our battle gear on, the sweat was pouring. Visions of white-walled, air conditioned radiology labs flitted through my thoughts as we trudged up to our objectives.

Second Squad was to provide security while First and Third each took one building. We had taken some sniper fire earlier in the day, and these two buildings looked like the possible hide spots of the sniper, so we were supposed to look for signs of that, I guess. I don't know why we just didn't take the buildings down, though.

Luckily, the snipers here sucked, so no one had been hit so far, knock on wood. I'd seen a few of our snipers with the battalion, and one of them supposedly had over 25 kills just on his last tour. He wouldn't have missed at only 200 meters, I'm sure.

Sgt Butler placed his teams in position as First and Third moved into clear their buildings. The Marines in my squad had to focus on what was out in the open and in other nearby buildings, but I watched the two target buildings instead, curious as to what the other squads might find. I really didn't expect them to find the sniper there, but I almost wished I was in there to see for myself. Almost.

When the blast came, I was taken my surprise. I dropped to the deck, more by instinct than by training. I could feel the

10

concussion of the second explosion wash over me. My ears were ringing, but I could still hear the calls of "Corpsman up!" cry out. It took me a moment to realize that that was me. I was the corpsman.

I started to get up, but hesitated. I knew I had to get over there, but my legs were like jelly. Another round exploded right in front of me, shrapnel zinging over my head. If I had stood up a moment ago, I would have taken all that shrapnel in my chest.

Before I left, I had promised Amy I would never be a hero, and I wanted nothing more than to just lie back down and hug the ground. But a second call rang out for me, and I knew what I had to do. I took a deep breath, then got up and ran, expecting another round at any second.

It seemed like forever, but I probably made it over to Cpl Deacon's team in just a few seconds, diving in just ahead of Sgt Butler. I landed so hard I knocked the breath out of me, and I gasped for air. When I looked up, I forgot all of that. I forgot everything, all my training, everything.

Cpl Deacon was lying down, holding what was left of his right leg. It was still attached, but from mid-thigh on down to his knee, it was hamburger. Blood pulsed through his fingers as LCpl Runolfson tried to put pressure on it. On the other side of him was the still form of Steve Potts, a newbie like me, just a few months in the Corps. Blood seeped from under his face-down body. Sitting up, but with blood making growing stains on his arm right arm and leg was Cy Pierce, a SAW gunner who bunked next to me in our SWA.

I froze. Rob Runolfson was covered in blood, but I didn't know if that was his or not. Cy was hurt, but maybe not too bad. I couldn't tell about Steve, but I knew Deacon was hurt bad.

"Come on, Doc. Get your ass in gear," Sgt Butler shouted as he pushed past me, joining Rob in applying pressure to Cpl Deacon's leg.

The tone of command in his voice must have registered, and I snapped back into corpsman mode. I saw that both of them had good pressure on Deacon, so I rushed to Steve. I felt for a pulse, not finding anything. I turned him over to give start CPR, but as I did, his head flopped to the side. His throat above his flak jacket had been torn open. He was gone. Only nineteen years old, and he left his life right there on the ground in the supposedly "safe" part of Ramadi. I looked up at Cy who motioned me to help our fire team leader. Blood was still seeping out with each beat of Cpl Deacon's heart, and his skin was taking on a grayish hue. He was conscious, but in shock.

I was aware of people behind me coming to help, but I knew I had to do something.

"When I tell you, I need both of you to let go. His femoral artery has been hit, and I need to close it," I told Rob and Sgt Butler.

Neither one of them argued with me, trusting me with what had to be done.

I snapped on a pair of latex gloves, took a deep breath, and said "Now!"

Both men let go and leaned back out of my way. Blood spurted up as I reached in with my hands to try and trap the artery. I knew what had to be done, but the artery was slippery and flailed like a garden hose. It took me several tries, but finally I caught it, almost yanking it out. Cpl Deacon groaned, but he didn't cry out as my hands rooted inside of him.

Carefully, I reached back into my kit and took out a hemostat. Just as carefully, I clamped it over the artery. I knew I had to be careful. The stupid thing could slip, causing a blowout. Cpl Deacon might have already lost too much blood already, but if it came loose, he would certainly bleed out.

HM2 Sylvester had been with the platoon commander, and he reached me first. He started to push me aside, but I was not budging. I could feel him looking over my shoulder before he grunted and started yelling for some Marines to act as stretcher bearers while he checked out Cy. I guess he figured that we could get Cpl Deacon back inside quicker than if a vehicle was sent out to get him.

"Listen, Cannon. You hold that hemostat and no matter what, don't let it slip. If it does, you get that artery clamped down, you hear me?" he said forcefully as he began to bandage Cy's wounds.

"I got it," I told him.

And I did. All the way to the aid station, stumbling over broken concrete and around barriers. I held on as we went across the water to Camp Ramadi and Charlie Med. I never let go until the surgeon there almost had to pry my fingers off of it.

Chapter 3

Hurricane Point
March 21, 2006

Tyson gurgled and cooed on the other end of the line. I knew he didn't have a clue as to what he was doing, but still, my little man's sounds made my heart pound.

"Did you hear him? Did you?" Amy asked as she took back the phone.

"I sure did, baby," I told her.

"He misses his daddy, don't you Tyson," she said before turning her attention back to me. "Anyway . . . what was I saying?"

"You were telling me about your checkups?"

"Oh yea, I was. Well anyway, the doctor said he's right in the middle of his percentile, no problems. He's strong as an ox and eating more and more. I'm fine, too. I'm still a little fat, but don't worry, I'll have that gone before you get back home."

"Baby, you're not fat. You were already almost down to normal before I left."

She hadn't been, really, but I knew what I was supposed to say. Her belly had been stretched pretty good by Tyson, and the muscles hadn't knitted back together by the time I deployed. But if that was the price to pay for him, I didn't have a problem with that.

"Anyway, Mom says that it took her almost a year after each one you was born."

When she said "Mom," I knew she meant my mom, not hers. We let the apartment go when I left to meet my new battalion at Twenty-Nine Palms prior to deployment, getting out of the lease thanks to the Soldiers, Sailors, Airmen, and Marines Relief Act, and she moved in with Mom so she could have help with Tyson. We gave Mom half of my VHA money, which she first refused, but with two extra people in her trailer, it came in handy. Amy saw her own mother once every couple of weeks or so even if they were only about 10 miles apart.

I let her chatter on, not really paying attention, but giving the appropriate grunts and comments. I couldn't help but feel good, just hearing her voice, hearing normalcy. Yesterday had been a wake-up call for me. My Iraq adventure became serious. I had lost someone, and while not really a close friend, he was still someone I knew well and liked. We were about the same age, and he was gone. Forever.

I had watched the day before as the Navy surgeon at Charlie Med took off Cpl Deacon's leg, a nurse putting it on a steel table to the side of the operating room like a piece of meat. I wasn't sterile, and in a stateside hospital, I would have been chased out. But I was there until I released my hold on the hemostat. When the surgical team moved in, I just backed away to the corner but didn't leave. I was afraid he wouldn't make it, he had lost so much blood. I was sure I had killed him by not acting sooner, by screwing up somehow.

The surgeon, though, wasted no time. After a quick assessment, he announced that the leg could not be saved. He went to work simply saving Deacon's life instead. They had suspended his mangled leg in a web of gauze that hung from a hook in the ceiling. After painting most of his body with what looked like Betadine, the loose skin and tissue was clipped with surgical scissors. Then the leg was sawn off with what was essentially a bone saw. The grating sound as the saw cut living bone made me wince. A chisel was used to clean up the area, then an electrocauterizer was brought into play, closing off arteries, veins, and nerves. With each zap, a smell that will live with me forever grew stronger. The nub was washed with a small sprayer, and it was only then that the surgeon closed off the leg. I knew what the procedure was and had seen photos of it in training. But seeing photos and actually being there were two different things. The smell, in particular, was not what I had expected.

It wasn't until he pronounced Deacon stable that I felt I could move. I had thought I was inconspicuous, back there in the corner, but as he finished, he looked over at me and nodded. The surgeon knew I had been watching—he knew I had to watch, and he had let me. Back at a stateside hospital, that would never have happened, me not being part of the team and not being sterile. But I guess he figured that with my hands inside of Deacons thigh, if I hadn't contaminated him yet, I never would.

They started to move Deacon to the ICU where he would wait until the casevac came to take him straight to Balad to await the flight to the Army hospital at Landstuhl. Charlie Med was a level 2 hospital, only concerned with saving lives. It was an Army hospital, but with only three physicians, none being surgeons, the Navy sent Charlie Surgical, a team of surgeons, to operate on the wounded. They handled lifesaving—more advanced medical work had to be done at Balad or Baghdad, the two level 3 hospitals in country.

I cleaned myself up the best I could, then went back to my SWA and lay down on my rack. I didn't get up when I heard the Black Hawk come in to take Deacon and probably Potts away. The helos that took away those killed were called "Hero Flights," and I'd heard that the company would be standing at attention when Steve's body was carried to the ambulance and then to the helo. I wasn't mentally ready for that, though, after watching the surgery. I just lay there, staring at the plywood ceiling of our squadbay, trying to find relief in sleep.

I spent most of the night like that, getting only snatches of sleep. When morning came around, the first thing I did was to call my Amy.

The phone companies and different groups donated calling cards to us, so it wasn't that difficult to call home if you could get a landline out. I called Amy every couple of days, but today, I really needed to hear her.

"Anyway, I told her that she had the temperature too high. It was going to burn the outside before the inside was cooked. She told me I was crazy, but you know, I was right. When she took it out, it was like stone cold inside, and she couldn't serve it. She should've listened . . . ."

Yesterday, I lost something inside of me, but listening to Amy's mundane chatter, well, that was putting something back in the tank.

"Uh, huh," I dutifully interjected, figuring I had another ten minutes left on the card, ten more minutes of the real world.

Chapter 4

The Government House, Ramadi
April 12, 2006

"All right, another day in paradise. We all know the drill, so keep alert. We've got that VIP visit here today," Sgt Butler told us as we took our positions on the roof of the Government House.

This was our third day of our rotation. There were some military folk stationed at the government compound, but no trigger pullers. Those were rotated in to provide outside security (the VIPs were protected inside by Triple Canopy, the contracting company made up mostly of ex-Recon, Special Forces, and SEALS). This was our first time with the duty, and frankly, it was pretty frustrating so far. We'd taken a daily dose of sniper fire, mortar fire, and even a couple of bursts of machine gun fire, but we hadn't had the chance to retaliate. There hadn't been a concerted attack.

That isn't to say there wouldn't be. We all knew that back in 2004, 12 Marines had been killed in the compound during a big coordinated Al Qaeda attack. Even without the big attack we all felt was coming, it was still pretty dangerous. The day before we rotated in, a Marine manning the gun on a hummer had taken an RPG round in the chest, right at the front gate. Then, last night, a rocket had hit the building with all the support staff, going right into the comm shack. The round tore up some of the radios, but the comm guy there was somehow untouched.

Food sucked worse than at Hurricane Point, and though we lived in a real building instead of a SWA, it might as well have been a SWA what with all the plywood and raw construction inside the buildings. Well, the Government House itself was kind of impressive, but we peons didn't do much there except for climbing up to the roof or providing security at the main entrance.

The worse thing, though, was that we shit and pissed in plastic bags that were then taken outside and burned. The place reeked, not only of the piss and shit, but of BO. Marines being Marines, put together a gym in one cramped corner of our building. It wasn't enough that we lived in a shithouse, but it also had the elements of a locker room thrown in, a locker room with no running water.

Lieutenant Hobbs was already on the roof when we got there. He probably got up there at zero-dark-thirty when Third Squad was on duty, and now he was going to sit up there with us. He was a new second lieutenant, very conscientious, but very green. Even I, one of the real newbies, recognized that. The guy needed to relax some, not be so serious. But he didn't bother me any, so how up-tight he was didn't really matter much to me. It was his funeral. He was the only black officer in the battalion, but that didn't seem to carry any weight with the brothers in the unit. The divide between officers and enlisted trumped race in the Corps, I guess.

Up on the roof, we had our squad, a sniper team, a fire support team, and some comm guys. We were just supposed to keep watch over the area. A bunch of the buildings around us had been taken down, but there were still buildings up that could act as hide spots for snipers, and there was enough rubble to hide a hundred insurgents. Some of the shot-up buildings already had names like the "Swiss Cheese" and "Battleship Gray."

I took my place under the netting that provided at least some shade. We had four hours before we would get relieved, and I intended on taking it easy. After only 20 minutes or so, I started nodding off. Taking it easy was one thing, nodding off was another. I had to get up and get moving. I went to the cooler and grabbed a handful of water bottles before going to each Marine and giving him one, telling him to keep hydrated. Preventive medicine had been hammered into us at FMSS, and it was not all just lip service. Heat stroke would take a Marine out of combat as readily as a bullet. I gave bottles to the comm guys, the lieutenant, and the sniper team, too.

The sniper was a strange-looking guy. Sitting on a rooftop dressed in one of their camouflaged suites, ghillie suits I think they were called, was weird enough. Was that supposed to make him invisible up here on top of the building? But even without the suit, he looked strange. There was nothing remarkable about his build. He was probably 5' 8" or 9" and about 160 lbs, give or take, not too buff or too skinny. But his head was somewhat fucked up. His ears were too big, and his eyes too small and too far apart. I could tell that he had some sort of syndrome, but I wasn't any sort of expert on that. I'd have to take a look online later or ask one of the docs. Whatever his condition, it obviously didn't affect him in shooting his rifle.

The other sniper, his spotter, was a complete 180. Tall, buff, and with a poster-boy square chin, he looked like what Hollywood imagined Marines should be. He smiled and thanked me for the water, unlike his buddy who took his without even a grunt.

Sniper teams were technically two people, but in Ramadi, they often went out in larger teams with the other members of STA to provide security and help observe the area. But up here on the roof with us, it was generally just the two man teams.

It was pretty quiet, but when we got word that the VIP was inbound, tension mounted. We didn't want to be the unit that lost some bigwig. I didn't have an assigned sector of fire, so I wandered over to stand by Sgt Butler at the edge of the roof to where I could look down at the entrance.

"You holding up OK, doc?" he asked me as I got up to him.

"Sure thing, Sarge," I told him.

He rolled his eyes at that but didn't say anything. I knew he didn't like to be called "sarge." I don't know if that was personal or a Marine thing, but there wasn't much else I could do to bust his chops. I may have been dressed in Marine Corps cammies, but that was only so I didn't stand out to any snipers. I was a "blue" corpsman, through and through, and I didn't want any of these grunts to forget that.

I knew I should probably lay off the sergeant, though. He was a good guy, a three-tour vet of Afghanistan and Iraq, and he knew his shit. If anyone could keep us alive, I knew he could. We'd already lost Steve, but God willing, that would be it.

"Secure your armor," he told me, pointing at my throat. "We need you safe if you're going to take care of us."

It was pretty hot up on the roof, and I had loosened the top of my flak jacket in an attempt to let some air circulate. I fastened up the Velcro, then took a glance over at him as he watched for the VIP convoy. That assistant sniper may look like a Hollywood Marine, but Sgt Butler just looked like a Marine, if that made sense. Physically, he looked fit, but not like some UFC fighter or bodybuilder. The scar across his chin was the only physical hint that he was a warrior. But his attitude, his focus, they left no doubt. This guy was a warrior through and through. I knew I was pretty lucky to have him as my squad leader.

"There they are," he said, pointing out to the first vehicles coming down Route Michigan, the main road in from Camp Blue Diamond.

The first vehicle was a gun hummer, and it stopped just the far edge of the gate to give cover. The next several vehicles entered the compound, pulling over to the side and parking. The fifth hummer, though, drove right on past the gate and started merrily on its way to no-man's land.

"What the fuck?" LCpl Jarod asked from his position a few meters down from me.

They must have been thinking that below us, too. We could hear the shouts as people started running around like crazy below us.

"Cpl Mays, heads up over there. I want eyes peeled. We've got a situation going on!" Sgt Butler ordered to the First Fire team leader as the lieutenant rushed over.

We lost sight of the wayward hummer, but the rest had stopped after two had pulled up just short of the gate. After a long, 30 seconds or so, the missing hummer backed up into view, swung about, and dashed into the compound. It zipped past some of the parked hummers, but a bit too close, taking the opening door of one hummer right off.

It skidded to a stop as a big Marine got out of the now doorless hummer and rushed over to meet it. I thought I could feel the volcano about to explode all the way up here. The big Marine, he had to be an officer, I just knew, opened the door to the hummer, and out came a short woman, whose laugh reach up to us. She wasn't pissed, but someone's ass was going to be grass, that's for sure. They stood around for a few moments talking, then all of them trooped into the Government House.

As the drivers and trigger pullers got out of their hummers, Sgt Butler said, to no one in particular, "No way! He got out already!"

He leaned over the edge and started to shout down, then seemed to think better of it.

"Mays, you've got it!" He turned to the lieutenant, "Sir, that's one of my buddies from 3/4. I'm going to go down and say hello for a bit. I'm leaving Cpl Mays in charge."

He rushed to the ladderwell, going down before the lieutenant could respond. I could tell the lieutenant wasn't happy about it, but he didn't say anything. It wasn't like every one of us was rooted in place for the entire four hours.

I looked back over the edge, and after a few moments, I could see Sgt Butler rush out. He must have flown down the stairs. He rushed over to behind one of the Marines and said something. The Marine turned around, and a series of back slaps and other manly means of greeting commenced. After a few moments, the two of them walked into the outbuildings, Sgt Butler obviously giving him the grand tour of our luxurious surroundings, and I lost sight of

Jonathan P. Brazee

them, at least until both of them came out onto the roof 15 minutes or so later.

Sgt Butler's friend was a big corporal who looked familiar, but it took me awhile to place him. He was the corporal who got hit by the IED back last month, the one I wheeled around to radiology. He looked none the worse for wear. He didn't seem to recognize me, so I didn't bother to re-introduce myself.

While we had our spurts of being targets for the insurgents, most of the time, it was pretty boring on the roof, so we settled into our routine. Whether it has anything to do with our VIPs downstairs or not, I don't know, but the routine changed when Gunny Tora, who had come up to make his rounds a few minutes before, left Rob and Cy and came up to the lieutenant.

"Lieutenant, we've got another looker,"

"Where at? Show me," he said as he jumped up, binos in hand.

I pulled out my own set of binos, trying to see the turkey-peeker. It took me a few minutes, but I finally saw him. Only he wasn't really a turkey-peeker; no up and down looks trying to watch us before dropping down into concealment. No, this guy was nonchalantly studying us. And he had to see that we were watching him.

The lieutenant watched for a few moments before ordering, "OK, get Cpl Lindt."

The sniper came up from the other side of the roof where he had been observing.

"We've got a looker over there, right on the roof of that building, about 90 mills to the left of the minaret," he said, holding three fingers up at arm's length "I want you to put a round beside him. Don't hit him, but let him know we'd rather not have him there."

"Aye, aye, sir," Cpl Lindt responded as he went to get his spotter.

I watched the two Marines as they moved to get into position. Remarkably, the Iraqi just stayed there, not moving as the sniper team set up. LCpl Poster Boy used some sort of a laser thing to get the range. At 876 meters, I figured that had to be a long shot, but they didn't seem to be concerned as they discussed things in sniper talk, all minutes and wind speed and such. The spotter looked like he was entering data on some sort of smart-phone looking thing, but the sniper seemed to be ignoring what the spotter was telling him. It probably took only a minute or so, but the Iraqi had plenty of time to boogie if we wanted to. But no, he just sat there, his head and shoulders clearly visible as he watched us. If he hadn't shifted his position a bit a few times, I would have sworn he was a dummy that the Iraqis had put up just to fuck with us.

Cpl Lindt reached under his blouse, took out something that looked like a round on a piece of chord, and put it in his mouth. After a calm "Send it" from his spotter, he aimed his rifle, let out a long breath, then fired. A second or two later, the round hit the stucco wall beside the Iraqi, and he disappeared from sight. Most of us broke out in laughter, and I heard on "Get some!" coming from my left.

Cpl Lindt started to get back up, mission accomplished, when to everyone's surprise the Iraqi made a second appearance.

"Well, Cpl Lindt, I guess your message didn't get through. Give him another, this time closer," the lieutenant ordered.

The sniper shrugged his shoulders and got back into position. He already had his dope, so within only a few moments, a second round was on its way downrange. This time, the stucco only inches from the Iraqi's head exploded into dust. Once again, the guy disappeared out of sight.

"That one's gotta hurt," the gunny said.

We all figured that the guy had to have gotten the message. We figured wrong. You could have knocked me over with a feather when he made another appearance, right in the same place. Was he a complete idiot? He had the glasses back up, and this time, it looked like he was talking on a cell phone or radio. That changed things. This was suddenly much more serious.

Several Marines called out to the lieutenant, but he had already seen the man for himself.

"Cpl Lindt, take him out now!"

It might have been funny before, but this was different. Talking on a radio could mean nothing good. Cpl Lindt drew down and sent the round downrange. A long second or two later, the round hit him square in the face, a pink bloody mist spraying out behind him, all clearly visible despite the distance. He collapsed in a heap. His binos fell onto the rooftop and bounce a few feet away from his outstretched hand. Half of his body was hidden from view, but the top half was out in the open, face up. We didn't need to go over and check him to know he was meat.

"Good job, Corporal," the lieutenant told the sniper.

The corporal merely shrugged. He had just killed a man, but he might just as well have bought a loaf of bread. Someone told me his nickname was Iceman, and I could see why. He tucked the tooth thing back inside his blouse, went over to the cooler and got a water for him and his spotter, then sat back down, pulling out a Three

Musketeers Bar out of his pocket for a for a nice little after killing snack.

Sgt Butler's guest left a few minutes after that, a little shaken, I could see. Well, the Marines were there to kick ass and take names, right? Cpl Iceman was just doing his job.

I had to admit, though, the guy kind of creeped me out.

Chapter 5

Ramadi
April 19, 2006

I tried to shift my weight. I never really felt at ease in the back of a hummer. The seat and the floorboards were too close together, so my knees came up too high. With all my battle gear, it was hard to get comfortable. Something or another was always digging into me. Of course, it was better than the alternative of humping everywhere. Lima Company had been out there on foot almost every day, patrolling between the High Water Bridge and the Low Water Bridge, the two bridges that crossed the Euphrates and led into the heart of the city from the north. When they humped, they carried about five tons of gear apiece. We'd done our share of foot patrols, too, going out at night and coming back in the morning, so uncomfortable or not, targets for IEDs or not, being inside a hummer gave me a bit more sense of security.

Today was part of the hearts and minds campaign. We were going out with a load of soccer balls, school supplies, and candy to give out, and I was going to be giving check-ups. We weren't supposed to fight, but I don't think anyone told the Iraqis that.

We pulled into a square and got out. The platoon had not been in any serious action since our first one last month. We'd been mortared and had pot shots taken at us, and two hummers had been blown up by IEDs, but no one was hurt. Even our first action was more of just being a target. We were probably the only platoon in the battalion that hadn't gotten into some serious shit yet. But this was still bad guy country, and except for Pacman, who was born-again and wanted to take every opportunity to convert the Iraqis, none of us wanted to be out here like this. We had to appear "friendly," as we were told.

Some Iraqis had already placed out some tables and chairs. I guessed they worked for us, but that doesn't mean any of us really trusted them. The chairs were full, mostly with women and children. They watched us pull up with flat eyes, neither welcoming nor antagonistic. Sgt Castanza was one of the first guys out, and he had a soccer ball in his hands. That got the interest of most of the kids. With full battle gear, he did that soccer thing where they keep kicking the ball up in the air, then converted that into a side kick, sending the ball slamming into the side of a building. The kids didn't even wait for their mothers' permission; they swarmed out of their chairs like a flock of birds and converged on the ball with shouts of "football, football!" in English. Their cries of delight sounded like the playground back home when I was a kid. Despite myself, I relaxed. It didn't seem likely that anyone would attack with all their kids around us.

Buster Seychik waved me over. He was Third Squad's corpsman, an HM3 on his second pump to the Sandbox.

"OK, HA Cannon, we need to set up. We've been all over this before, but mostly what we can do is just triage."

Buster was a little too gung ho for me, too Marine. He wore his FMFEWS, or Fleet Marine Force Enlisted Warfare Specialist Device, like it was his most prized possession. Most junior corpsmen, and that included HM3s, were on a first name basis with each other, but he was always HA this and HM that. I even heard him call Terry Banks, over in First Platoon, "HM3 Banks" before, someone not only his own rank, but his good friend. He was a pretty good guy for all of that and knew what he was doing.

"Without that female medic coming, we can't treat any women here, but little girls we can, depending on what's wrong with them."

We didn't have any female corpsmen with the battalion, so we were supposed to get a loaner from the 228th, the National Guard unit that controlled most of the city, to take care of any Iraqi women who came for treatment. The medic never showed, though.

Even though this was the 100th time I had heard it today, he was right, though. We were corpsmen, not doctors or medical assistants. I had been trained to save a life in the field and to take simple sick call, but my clinical skills were pretty lacking. We'd give out antibiotic cream, dress wounds, and give out the kind of over-the-counter meds anyone could buy back at Wal-Mart, but that was about it. If someone was in serious shape, we could casevac him or her back to base, but that caused a shitload of problems, so we had been told in no uncertain terms that that was a last resort.

A civilian translator came up to us and asked, "You are the doctors? Please, come with me," in heavily accented English.

I guess all our Iraqi translators were civilians, but the ones who were assigned to us wore uniforms and battle gear. This was a middle-aged man dressed in grey slacks and a white shirt. He gestured with his arm towards one of the buildings. I looked at Buster and he looked at me. I didn't really think we needed to be going into a building alone, and even gung ho as Buster was, he didn't think so, either. We shouldn't have worried. Sgt. Butler had our six.

"Mays!" he called out. "Get your team and clear that building there, then provide security for the docs."

Cpl Mays looked sort of looked and sounded like Bubba Blue, Forest Gump's friend who was going to open up the shrimp restaurant after the war. The other Marines sometimes started going into all the ways to cook shrimp when he was around. But unlike Bubba, Mays was no dummy. After Sgt Butler, Mays was probably the most competent Marine in the squad, so I was glad it would be his team with us.

We let him clear the building, then when he gave us the OK, the two of us went inside. Whoever had set this up had a unique idea of an examining room. There was a folding table in the back of the main room and two chairs. Period. Nothing else.

Buster just sighed and told me to take the chair on the right side while he took the one on the left. He told our translator to start bringing in the patients. For the next hour or so, we saw kids. No men came, and without the female medic, no women, at least for treatment. All the kids had who I assumed were their mothers with them. I checked runny noses, coughs, infected cuts—pretty much everything we could have expected. I gave out what medicine I had, telling the mothers the dosages through the translator. Everyone listened to me with rapt attention as if I was some sort of expert. In reality, though, except for a broken finger than I splinted, everything I did could have been done by any mother back in the US. This was basic medicine.

I hoped I wasn't hurting anyone by giving them the wrong treatment. I may be a corpsman and not an MD, but the "doing no harm" part still held true for me. I wanted to help, but the hard part was that these were not Marines. Marines might want to hide what was wrong with them so they could stay in the fight, but at least they spoke English and would answer to direct questions. These kids didn't speak English, were mostly scared, and weren't sure how to react to me. I had the translator, but I didn't get the feeling that he was that good. I would ask a detailed question, and he would speak to the kid or the mother for all of five seconds before coming back to me with an answer. I knew if I was back at Kaiser Permanente in San Diego that most of my patients would speak English, of course, but maybe I just wouldn't be very good with kids whether in Ramadi or San Diego.

When the old man was led in, his arm on top of that of a young, fully-robed woman, things were a little different. He sat down, silent and motionless. The girl spoke to the translator who then told me that they wanted me to restore the old man's sight. I started to tell them I was only a corpsman, but I thought I might as well look. I knew in some countries simple, easily-removed cataracts caused blindness, and maybe we could get him into a surgeon.

I tilted the old man's chin up and looked into his eyes, or the ruins that were left of them. Something had eaten away the corneas and destroyed the pupils themselves. Aqueous humor was clearly apparent and murky. The right eye was eaten away past the lens, and the left was not much better. It didn't look like what I remembered about trachoma, a disease about which we had been briefed as it was prevalent here. That would not have destroyed the eyes like this. What had eaten away his eyes, well, I didn't know. But I did know that he would never see again.

I told the translator that there was nothing to be done, but before he could repeat that in Arabic, the old man simply stood up, holding his arm out for his escort. She took it and the two of them marched out, but not before I caught the full brunt of her glare, coming from above her veil. It wasn't my fault that something had happened to him, that there was nothing I could do. Nothing anyone could do, for that matter. But somehow, I felt that I had failed.

The next patient came up while I was still watching the man walk out of the building, standing tall and proud. I turned back to see a small girl of about four years old. With one hand in her mother's, she held up the other arm to me. Her right arm was bandaged with a piece of cotton, blood staining it with little red flowers.

She was much older than Tyson, but something in her eyes made me think of him. Maybe it was the trust that I was going to help her. I felt a little wave of paternal instinct.

"Well, what have we here?" I asked, leading her to sit on the chair.

I knew she didn't understand a word I said, but I hoped my tone was comforting enough. I carefully unwrapped the bandage until her arm was bare. Right in the meat of her forearm, a piece of jagged metal stuck out. I didn't need to ask: I knew it was shrapnel, and while it could have come from anyone, I figured it was ours.

"The mother says the girl was hurt yesterday when the Americans attack. The American army bomb hit the street and came in the house. It killed their cat," the translator said.

I looked up at the last. What had their cat to do with the price of tea in China?

He simply shrugged before continuing, "That is what she says. They tried to take the metal away, but the father says the Americans put it there, so the Americans must take it away."

This was actually something I could do. I was trained to render aid to wounded Marines; she was not much different, only smaller. I cleaned up her arm, careful not to move the shrapnel. It looked embedded pretty deeply, but I was more worried about infection. I took out a hypodermic, and the girls eyes got big. She didn't cry, though. I told the translator to tell her it was going to be like a bee sting.

I gave her the first shot, and while tears welled up in her eyes, she still didn't cry. Her mother, though, looked like she might faint. I wished we had another chair so she could sit down. I didn't need her to pass out on me.

Once her arm was numb, I took a pair of forceps and slowly eased the piece of metal out of her arm. My maneuvering started the bleeding again, but I flushed the wound out several times with both water and Betadine before stitching it up. I was kind of proud of my needlework. Amy was a big seamstress at home, making clothes and things, and she wouldn't have been able to fault my work.

Normally, a basic corpsman is not authorized to give out things like antibiotics, but in wartime, things have a habit of shifting. I had been given several Z Paks and some Augmentin before I came out, but while the Z Paks were pretty good meds, I thought the Augmentin would be better for a wound like this. I took out two tablets and used my pill cutter to cut each one into fourths. I told her mother to make sure she took one piece twice a day and to use it all up.

I waited while the translator did his thing, then stepped back— my signal that the treatment was over. The little girl slid off the chair and shyly took the sucker I held out to her. She gave it a tentative lick, then quickly put it into her mouth, jaws working with pleasure. The mother, who had not let go of her daughter's left arm during the entire procedure, leaned over and said something to her.

The little girl looked up, took the sucker out, and softly said "Shakran," before putting the candy back into her mouth.

By instinct, I started to reach out to tousle her hair, but stopped, trying to remember if that was one of the cultural taboos here. Maybe I should have paid more attention to our Arabic culture classes back at Lejeune.

Jonathan P. Brazee

I had treated a couple more minor cases, nothing serious, when Buster called me over.

"HA Cannon, what do you think about this?" he asked, pointing to a teenage boy who was sitting listlessly on the chair. He stepped back to allow me to get a better look.

The kid was probably 14 or 15, and I could immediately tell he was in pretty bad shape. His skin color was sallow, and he was breathing in quick, shallow breaths. I took his wrist and almost dropped it. He was burning up. His pulse was weak and febrile. I pinched his fingertips; his perfusion was slow. Whatever else was ailing the boy, he was severely dehydrated.

I looked up at his face. Dull, listless eyes stared back at me. It looked like he had given up and was only waiting to die.

I was at a loss, though. I'm not sure what Buster wanted me to say. I could treat obvious injuries, I could treat normal common diseases. I was not a doctor, though, and I was not a diagnostician.

"Give him an IV?" I offered. That would help with the dehydration, at least.

"Yea, but what's wrong with him?"

I looked at the boy's parents who were waiting anxiously. I knew the man could have been laying IEDs last night, but now, he was merely a father afraid for his son. I looked at the translator as if he could suddenly diagnose patients. Finally, I had to look back at Third Squad's corpsman.

"I don't know," I admitted.

Buster smiled and clapped my shoulder. "Of course you don't know," he said. "We're corpsmen, the first line of treatment. But it's important that we never overreach ourselves. We can see that this boy is going to die soon, maybe within hours, if he doesn't get treatment, but as to what is wrong with him, we can guess, but that won't do our patients any good. They need full medical treatment, and we need to know when we can't do any more and to push cases like this up to the MDs back at camp. We need to know our limitations."

Of course he was right. I remembered our training about standard of care, what we were allowed to do and what we weren't. I knew Buster had been testing me, but I hadn't realized the focus of his test. OK, lesson learned.

Buster asked Cpl Mays to send a runner to get the lieutenant. He then told the parents, through his translator, that the boy needed immediate attention back at the hospital or he would die. It was easy to tell when the translator got to the point about the boy dying.

The father took a step back while the mother gasped, putting her arms around the neck of the unresponsive boy.

Lieutenant Hobbs came in with SSgt White, the platoon sergeant. Where the lieutenant was all serious earnestness, the platoon sergeant was a gruff, surly Marine who liked to do things his way, not by the book. He was over the weight limitations and was constantly on weight control, but he could hump all day, half carrying fitter-looking Marines when they faltered.

"What do you have, doc?" the platoon commander asked Buster.

"Sir, this boy here," he started, pointing to the kid, "is pretty bad off. I'd say he's got only a couple hours left. Back at Charlie Med, they might be able to save him. I think we need to get him there."

"Remember what happened up at Haditha, sir," SSgt White reminded the lieutenant.

At Haditha, the Marine CO had authorized life-saving treatment for a little Iraqi girl. She had to remain hospitalized, and some of the local bigwigs took offense at that. It had caused a pretty big brouhaha, and consequently, we had all been warned about taking in strays. We hadn't been ordered not to do it, but we needed to use extreme discretion.

The lieutenant nodded, then asked Buster, "Charlie Med? Can't our docs at Hurricane Point help him?"

I understood the lieutenant's point. Charlie Med was the hospital over at Camp Ramadi, the main base in the city. It was "owned" by the National Guard. Our small aid station was under our control, and that gave us more leeway in how we handled things.

"No sir. I don't think we have the treatment capabilities ourselves. He probably needs to go to Baghdad or Balad, but there's no way he should be moved that far. He needs treatment, and fast. Like within an hour."

2ndLt Hobbs didn't look convinced. He looked up at the mother of the boy who looked back with hopeful eyes. She couldn't understand what was being said, but I think she understood that the decision on what to do with the boy was in the platoon commander's hands.

When it looked like the lieutenant was wavering, SSgt White said, "Remember what the skipper said. Do we really want to get into all that political shit?"

The lieutenant was a serious man, not given much to displays of emotions. But since taking over the platoon, it was pretty obvious that he cared for us. Not a show of caring, not merely acting in order to get us to follow him, but real caring. He was a compassionate person.

I could see him come to a decision, and I was pretty sure that we were going to try to save the boy's life. He just started to say something when an Iraqi rushed in, shouted out a few words of Arabic, then ran back out.

Whatever he said had an immediate effect. All the Iraqis, translators included, quickly got up and rushed to the door. All of them. The father of the dying boy picked up his limp son and joined the exodus.

SSgt White beat all of them to the punch, though. As soon as the people started getting up, with a single "Shit!" he rushed out the door, the first one out of the building. I could hear him bellowing to the platoon to get ready.

"But sir!" Buster shouted at the boy's father, regardless of the fact that the man did not understand English. "If he doesn't get treatment, he's going to die!"

The man ignored him. His wife did look back at us with a troubled look on her face, but she joined her husband and son in getting out of the room.

"Cpl Mays, wrap it up here and get to the vehicles," the platoon commander ordered before he rushed out as well, pushing past Iraqis who were still trying to get out.

I had taken off my battle gear to treat the patients. Orders were to keep it on at all times, but I thought treating kids looking like that wouldn't be conducive to getting their trust, so off it had come. I scrambled now to get it back on.

Buster, Cpl Mays' team, and I followed the last of the Iraqis out. Outside, the place was rapidly getting deserted. There were a few backs still visible as every Iraqi tried to make himself scarce.

"I don't like this shit," Jerry Scanlon muttered, the fire team's SAW gunner.

I grunted my agreement. If the hajiis scattered like this, that usually meant something was up. While we went out on purpose to close with and kill the enemy, this time, we were out on a humanitarian mission. I could see the lieutenant on the radio while SSgt White tightened up our defensive posture. I even unslung my M16 and scanned the buildings, waiting for them to hit us.

2ndLt Hobbs put down the radio and gave us the hand signal to mount up. I felt a surge of relief as I rushed to my hummer. We weren't out of the woods yet. The Iraqis had run for a reason, and that reason could hit us at any time.

I think we were ready to roll in record time. Our route back had already been planned. It was not the same route as we had taken on the way in. We pulled out and made our way through the buildings, each one capable of hiding a hundred Al Qaeda insurgents.

After about five minutes, I heard the whup-whup of an Apache making a pass over us. In many ways, being a Marine battalion in a National Guard's area of operations made things difficult for us, but in this case, I was glad of it. An Apache was a pretty serious helo, more lethal than the Marine's Cobra. It even looked fierce.

Whether it was because of the Apache overwatch or us taking a different route back, we made it to Hurricane Point without being hit. Something had gone down, though, but we never found out what it was.

I often wondered later about the fate of the teenage boy. Intellectually, I knew he must have died later that day or night. I never even knew his name.

Chapter 6

Hurricane Point
April 22, 2006

"You going to the gym, doc?" Jerry asked as we walked back from chow.

"Fuck you," I responded without rancor.

"Come on, get rid of that baby fat!"

"We just went on a 12-hour patrol, I'm tired, and I want to catch some z's," I said. "I'm hitting the rack.

"OK, OK. If you don't want to be a lean, green fighting machine, that's up to you," he said, flexing his biceps in a beach pose. "Me, I'm gonna get me some iron before I hit the rack."

I watched him peel off and head to the gym. This wasn't Lejeune where people got into PT gear to exercise. Most Marines simply took off their blouse and had at it.

I hadn't been kidding. Last night's patrol sucked. We humped around all night, first as "camouflage" for dropping off a five-man sniper team at their hide, then making "house calls" on addresses given to us by the IPs, the Iraqi police. And we got into the shit again, for the second night in a row. We went into one house and the owner fought back, coming out of a room with an AK. He was taken down, but Steve Jenner was hit. I had gone into the house to treat him, but I couldn't get my eyes off of the Iraqi man. He had taken four or five rounds dead center in his chest and was laying face-up on the floor of the room. His room, his house. I wondered if he was really an insurgent or just some hothead who didn't want armed men tramping through his home. The IPs, though, thought he was an insurgent, one of the bomb makers. Bad guy or not, this was the first dead Iraqi I had seen up close and personal.

I bandaged up Jenner's arm and he went back into the fight. He wouldn't even consider going back, so I quit trying to suggest it and just told him to get his arm dressed at the battalion aid station when we got back.

I was looking forward to a shower and sleep as I walked back to our SWA. Before I got there, I came up on Rick Haddad, dressed in the oh-so fashionable shorts, t-shirt, flip-flops, towel around the shoulder, and full battle gear that told me he had just come back from the showers himself. I didn't think I would ever get used to that ensemble, even when I was wearing it. There was something about flip-flops and flak jackets that just didn't jive.

He was in some sort of argument with two other Marines. Rick was a lance corporal in the squad's Third Fire Team. He was pretty mouthy and rather irreverent. Where other Marines ran around with their lusty "Oorahs," his was a more sarcastic version of it, something that pissed some people off. He was a good Marine in the field, though, tough as nails.

He was also a Lebanese-American, and that earned him some grief at times. He didn't speak Arabic, only the handful of words that all of us learned. He wasn't Muslim. But that didn't stop others from giving him shit about it, calling him "raghead" and stuff like that.

I didn't know if whatever was going on was because of his mouth, his being Arab-American, or what, but it looked like he was giving as good as he was getting. He was up in the face of one of the other Marines, a guy a good four inches taller than him. They were both posturing up, and the third Marine hovered off Rick's shoulder, adding to the shouting.

I just wanted to get back to my SWA, so I kept walking. Whatever it was, it was not my fight. Until the taller Marine gave Rick a shot in the chest that knocked him down, that is.

Rick was a tough son-of-a-bitch, so that had to have been a pretty good shot. He immediately jumped up and tackled the other guy, driving him to the ground. The third guy jumped on the pile and started pounding the back of Rick's head while Rick wailed away on his opponent.

I looked around for an officer or staff NCO, but even for such a small camp, no one was in sight. I looked back at the three fighters, and the second guy had pulled Rick back with a headlock, giving the tall guy a chance to scramble up and begin to pound on Rick.

I've never been much of a fighter. My one school fight was back in 5th grade when Justin Marks and I squared off over him taking my french fries during lunch. If I said it was a draw, well, that would have been generous with regards to my efforts. And I certainly did not want to be drawn into some stupid Marine macho shit. But Rick was getting it handed to him, and he was one of my squad mates.

With trepidation, I lowered my head and charged the three men, knocking the tall guy back off of Rick. He seemed surprised. That, or just the force of my rush, threw him flat, and somehow, I landed on top of him. I didn't waste any time but started flailing away on the guy, punching as hard as I could. I probably got in half a dozen blows when he twisted, pushing me off to the side. I kept swinging, but I couldn't really connect in that position. He got up to his knees, and now he was swinging. I tried to ward off the blows, but he connected two or three times in a row, and my face exploded.

I went crazy. I never felt that way before, but all I wanted to do was to kill the guy. Knowing Rick, this guy could have been in the right, but I didn't care. When he smashed my nose, I lost all reason. I kicked and swung, all from my back. I don't know if I connected, but if I didn't, it wasn't for lack of trying.

I felt hands grabbing me by the back of my flak jacket, pulling me off the guy. I turned and swung at my new assailant, connecting solidly on his chin. I was about to swing again when to my horror, I realized I had just hit Gunny Tora, our company gunny. I had just struck a staff NCO!

That knocked the fight out of me. I stared at him in shock.

"All of you, stop this shit!" he shouted, still holding me. "You!" he shouted at the tall Marine. "Who are you?"

"Uh, LCpl Whitten, H & S Company," he told gunny, wiping his forearm across his nose.

I was in it deep, but still, I felt a thrill. I had connected with him.

"And you?"

"LCpl Thierry, Gunny. H & S Company," said the second guy.

"You two, get back to your company CP. Report to Gunny Miller and tell him to hold you there until I get there."

"Aye-aye, gunny," they said in unison.

Thierry picked up his helmet, which had come off, and the two hurried off. Gunny looked back at us with fire in his eyes.

"What the fuck do you two dipwads think you're doing? How about saving some of that for the fucking hajiis!"

I stared at his cheek, which was turning red where I had hit him. I was waiting for the explosion and charges.

He let go of me. "Both of you, get back to your hootch and don't move a muscle until Sgt Butler gets there."

"But, . . ." I started. I had just hit him. I knew the consequences of that.

"You got something to say, Cannon? Something other than that you two got into a fight with other Marines? That you stopped when I came up?"

I could see the swelling already start on his face. He knew I had hit him, but he also knew what would happen if he reported that. I couldn't believe it. He was giving me a break!

"No Gunny! Nothing to say!"

"OK, the two of you, I want to see asses and elbows. Get to your hootch now!"

He didn't have to tell us twice. Both of us took off at a run, and we didn't stop until we were back.

"You OK, man?" Rick asked.

I didn't even know, to be honest. But sitting on the edge of my rack, I took inventory. I'd had my battle gear on, so it would have been pretty hard to get to hurt, but my nose was swollen and beginning to ache. My hand hurt, too. I must have punched Whitten in the helmet or something.

"No, I'm all right," I answered.

"That was pretty righteous, you know?" he said.

"I don't know. I think I hit him once or twice, but it looks like he got me better."

"Not that. I mean you were righteous, taking that big guy on like that, Doc."

When I didn't say anything, he went on, "I mean, I thought you weren't much on fighting. You're not too aggressive, if you know what I mean. Like you're only putting in your time here."

I thought about it for a second. Why had I joined the fight? I was not a fighter by nature. As corny as it sounded to me, I think it all had to do with that Marine Corps *esprit de corps,* about brotherhood. Rick could be an annoying loudmouth, but as one of my squadmates, he was *our* annoying loudmouth.

"Eh, I couldn't let you have all the fun, you know," I said, unwilling to get all mushy and sentimental.

"Well, you're not too bad for a squid," he said with a laugh.

"If you two are done with your love fest, maybe you can tell me what just happened? Gunny just tore me a new asshole."

We both jumped when Sgt Butler stepped out in front of us. We'd never heard him come up.

"Ah, well, nothing, you know, Sergeant, nothing happened. Just a misunderstanding," Rick stammered out.

"Nothing my ass. Haddad, you've got to keep that trap of your closed. Learn some friggin' discipline!"

"But, ..."

"But nothing. You're lucky the gunny is letting me take care of this, not the CO. How would you like a summary court instead?"

I gulped, I mean physically gulped. That was pretty serious stuff. That could result in 30 days in the brig at Fallujah.

"And you, Doc, what the heck do you think you were doing? You're supposed to heal people, not mess them up." He paused a

Jonathan P. Brazee

moment, then his tone lightened up. "Did you really tackle the biggest one of them?"

"I guess so. The other one was on his back, and that guy, he was the only one I could get to."

"We've got ourselves a warrior-doc, there Haddad. I think we'll make a Marine of him yet."

With that, he spun around and started to leave. "You've got the shit burning detail next week at the government center. Not just for us, but for the entire installation," he shouted out over his shoulder. "Enjoy!"

Chapter 7

Government Center, Ramadi
April 26, 2006

"What, you'd think we've both got cooties or some shit," Rick said as we walked into the building.

"I think 'shit' is the operative word," I said as we both broke into laughter.

Living in the government center was an assault on anyone's nose, but with us given the duty of burning the plastic bags of shit, well, I would guess we were pretty pungent. Our noses might have become deadened to the smell a bit, but judging from the way others avoided us, I imagine we were pretty ripe.

The first floor of the Government House itself was still pretty impressive despite every window being sandbagged. The ceiling had to be 20 feet high, and the big staircase leading up to the second deck could have doubled as some billionaire's stairway. The ladders we took to get up to the roof were not as impressive, but that first one sure was.

A bulletin board had been put up on the second deck, and out of habit, we checked it. Different word tended to be passed there.

"Check this out. They want suggestions for the company t-shirts," Rick said, pointing to one piece of paper.

I edged over to look.

The first one to catch my eye was "Fuck with us and we'll fuck with you!"

"Eh, I don't think the CO will accept that one," I said with a laugh.

Captain Wilcox was a tough mother, but a born-again Christian, or at least a pretty devout guy, and he didn't accept swearing by his Marines. Personally, I think he was trying to hold back the flood with the proverbial finger in the dyke. Back in the real world, I was never much of a guy for swearing and stuff, but out here in the Sandbox, everyone, and I mean everyone cursed. It's "fuck this" and "shit that." I think even the chaplain probably lets out a "shit" or two.

"Here's a good one," Rick said, pointing.

"Kilo Company: Killed More People Than Cancer."

"Oh, man, that's cold," I said.

Jonathan P. Brazee

"You know, I bet we can come up with something if we tried," he said, excitement rising in his voice.

"Yea, like 'Come to Iraq and Burn Your Shit'!" I said.

"No, I'm serious. We could do it," he insisted.

"Well, we'd better do it up on the roof. We were supposed to get up there as soon as we finished with the detail."

"Yea, but think about it, OK?"

We turned away and started up the smaller ladder to go up another floor. Rick and I had started hanging out, not just on the shit detail, but during our free time. I even asked Sgt Butler if I could move with Third Fire Team during our patrols. We couldn't BS while on patrol, of course, but it felt good knowing he had my six.

Rick was from Longmont, Colorado. He'd been born there after his parents had left Lebanon as refugees. His father had worked for the Marines and had been in the barracks in Beruit when they had been bombed. After that, his dad had requested asylum, and it had been granted. Rick grew up a typical Colorado kid, worshipping the Broncos and living each winter on skis. His parents moved to Dearborn during his senior year in high school, but he had stayed with a friend until graduation. He spent a semester at the Colorado School of Mines before deciding that school wasn't for him, so he enlisted.

Despite his fatal flaw of being a Broncos fan, we actually had a lot in common. And even while surrounded by the shit smoke, I didn't regret coming to his aid one bit. It was a pretty good thing to have a friend.

As we came out onto the roof, we had to endure the expected jibes: "It's the shit brothers," "You smell like crap," "Can't you get your shit together?"

"Ha, ha, ha," Rick responded in a deadpan voice. "That is so funny, I don't know when I'll stop laughing."

He went to his position while I relieved Buster, who had stayed on with my squad while I was burning shit. The Marines had to have coverage all the time, and he hadn't batted an eye about staying an extra 45 minutes. That amount of time might not seem like much, but when it took away from maybe 45 minutes of sleep, it took on a different perspective.

I thanked him, then sat down to inventory my kit. I hadn't wanted it around me while I was on the detail for fear of contamination, so now that I was on duty, I wanted to make sure I had everything I might need. This was our third time at the center, and so far, I had done nothing more than sick call. We'd been hit quite often, but it seemed more like harassing fire. India, though, had taken some shit last week. They'd had to casevac one of their staff sergeants to Balad and off to Lansdstuhl after he'd taken some serious shrapnel from a mortar round up here on the roof. A couple of other guys had been hit, too, but nothing very serious.

"You starting any more fights there, Doc?" Sgt Butler asked as he came up.

"Who me, Sarge? Never in a million years!"

"Good. We don't need you taking out any of our Marines. You just be ready for the call of 'Medic up!'"

Since I started calling him "Sarge," he had started to retaliate by referring to me as a "medic." Buster had overheard him do it and wanted to go correct him. No Navy corpsman is a "medic," and Buster, full of righteous fury, was going to set my squad leader straight. I had to pull him back and assure him that Sgt Butler was just pulling my chain, that is was an inside joke. Buster huffed and puffed, then said it wasn't funny and that NCO's shouldn't be joking with E2's. He left it alone, though.

"Vehicle approaching down Michigan," La'Ron Talbot called out.

Sgt Butler joined SSgt White as they made their way to the north side of the roof. I decided to follow.

"Yea, looks like it's that reporter coming to cover the conference," my squad leader said.

"Where was he from? What did the lieutenant say? *The NY Times*?" asked SSgt White.

"Not the lieutenant. That WM major. But yes, that's where he's from. Too late to the party, though. Only six of the provincial ministers showed up. Six out of 36. They've already taken off, leaving the gov here to man the fort alone," Sgt Butler said.

"'Man the fort alone?' With a company of Marines, Triple Canopy, that SEAL team that came in, and what, 50 or 60 others? He's hardly alone."

"You know what I mean, staff sergeant. The sheiks here, they won't give him the time of day 'cause he's a commoner. His ministers keep getting knocked off. Al Qaeda's tried to do him, what 30 times now? But that doesn't stop him. He keeps coming in to work each day like he's the governor of Delaware, not Al Anbar."

I looked up at Sgt Butler in a little bit of a new light. I knew he was a kick-ass Marine. I didn't know he was looking into all the politics in all of this. Like most everyone else, I really didn't pay too much attention to that. I knew we were in Sunni land, and I knew the Shia and the Sunnis were going at it when they weren't going after us. After that, I really didn't care much. Even if we went out

Jonathan P. Brazee

and gave out soccer balls and treated sick Iraqis, I still had the mentality that it was us versus them. And by them, I meant all of them, all Iraqis.

"Ah, whatever. He's still just a raghead as far as I'm concerned," SSgt White said while we watched the reporter get escorted into the building.

Sgt Butler looked like he wanted to say something, but he just shrugged his shoulders and kept quiet.

Here at the government center, we had civil affairs Marines, guys whose job it was to help build up the country. They lived in this shithole, getting mortared and shot at every day. And for what? To help the Iraqis. We had the governor, coming in to the government center each day, risking himself just to show a degree of normalcy to his constituents. If all Iraqis were the same, that they wanted to take out their own governor, then what the fuck were we doing here?

We were spending lives and taxpayers money because we thought that they were not all the same. We helped Japan and Germany rebuild after WWII. They had been our enemies, and now they were among our strongest allies. I hoped our efforts here in Iraq would have the same degree of success.

A huge explosion broke my train of thought. Smoke billowed not 100 yards from the gate. The hummer that had brought the reporter must have been hit. It was rare for vehicles to travel Michigan alone just for this reason. There was no support. On the roof, we all got ready. Below us, down in building we called home while we were here, Second Platoon, the Quick Reaction Force, would be getting ready to dash out if needed.

Just as 2ndLt Hobbs rushed up to the roof, we could see the four Marines from the hummer walking back down Michigan as if nothing had happened. One looked back, then we could see him laugh as he slapped another of them on the shoulder.

It seemed surreal to me that these Marines could be so nonchalant about getting blown up. I understood gallows humor, but there were even pools put together, $10 to enter, on who would have the most vehicles blown up underneath him by the time we rotated back to Lejeune.

The sun was already going down, so it wasn't murderously hot, but still, I need to keep the Marines hydrated. I swear some of them didn't have enough sense to drink when they needed to. I started grabbing water bottles and distributing them.

Cpl Dunlop, the new Second Fire Team leader, took all of this team's water when I came up. He had come over from First Platoon after Cpl Deacon had been casevac'd. He hadn't done any of the workups with us, so he kept doing things like this so Runolfson and Pierce (who was back to full duty after taking shrapnel in his arm and leg) knew he was in charge. It had been over a month now, so I thought he was going a bit too far. He was a new corporal, true, but he could take some lessons from Mays and Choi, the other two fire team leaders.

As I was giving out the water, HM2 Sylvester came to the roof. I saw him come up, and I was glad I was doing something when he came instead of just sitting on my ass.

HM2 Sylvester was the First Squad and platoon corpsman both. I wasn't sure how much influence he had on my next duty station, or if it was Senior Chief (or even 2ndLt Hobbs, for that matter.) But I figured if I wanted to get into C School, I needed to keep him impressed.

Sylvester was like Buster in some ways. He was a die-hard "green" corpsman, mighty proud of his FMFEWS. He had never served with the Navy, from what I had heard. He didn't look like what most people would expect of someone who served with the Marines, though. He reminded me of a penguin, to be honest, from his penguin shape to his waddle when loaded down with his battle gear. He had a Silver Star, though, from the initial invasion back in 2003. I'd only heard rumors about what he'd done to get it, but he'd also earned a Purple Heart at the same time, so it must have been pretty hairy. Medal or not, the guy had the undying respect of the Marines in the platoon. Even the lieutenant and SSgt White gave him his dues.

He sat down on an MRE box, then motioned for me to sit as I finished passing out the water.

"Everything going OK?" he asked.

"Not bad. You know Pacman, I mean PFC Lopez, is down with a heavy cough and sore throat, but the rest, everyone's OK. No issues."

"Yes, I checked with Lopez an hour ago. I think he'll be fine in a day or so."

Pacman was down in our berthing spaces. I hadn't seen any reason to get him back to Hurricane Point.

"You know, you're doing a pretty good job, Zach. There was some concern with you being only an HA, and we had a chance to bring in an HM from India after your fight with the H & S Marines, but Sgt Butler said he'd just as soon have you as his corpsman."

This was news to me. Very welcome news. I was surprised and more than a little touched that Sgt Butler would stick up for me.

"Have you thought about working on your FMFEWS?" he asked, much to my surprise.

"Uh, HM2, I, uh, well . . . I'm glad you think I can qualify, but really, after this tour, I want C School to be a radiology tech. I'm not really cut out to be an FMF Corpsman."

There was a pause as Sylvester looked off in the distance. I hoped I hadn't pissed him off saying I didn't want to be stay with the Corps.

"Don't sell yourself short, Zach. You are cut out for it. Sgt Butler is a pretty good judge of character, and from what I've seen, from what Buster has seen, what Terry Banks has seen, well, we are all in agreement on that."

Buster Seychiik was a recruiter at heart, so that didn't surprise me. But Terry Banks was not FMFEWS qualified, nor did he want to be. He was anxious to get back to the Navy side of medicine.

"Well, anyway, just think about it."

He stood up, hitched up his flak jacket, and left, disappearing down below. I really had no intention of going native. I had to admit, that while much of Ramadi sucked, being with the Marines was not as bad as I had expected. I would still rather be back at Balboa Naval Hospital, back with my family, back with a clean room and good chow. But if I had to be out here in the middle of the desert getting shot at by radical insurgents, I'd probably not be able to find a better group of guys to be with.

I looked over to Rick as he glassed the area around the government center. I had a feeling that he and I would be friends for long, long time. I would never have met him if I hadn't been assigned to the Marines, to 3/8 in particular.

I looked at my watch. Another 90 minutes and we'd be done up here for eight hours. Eight hours to see if there was any hot chow, eight hours to try and clean up. Eight hours to sleep. I knew some of the other companies did eight hours on and 16 off, but Capt Wilcox thought eight hours on made us lose our focus. So we did the four on and eight off instead.

Some previous battalions even had their companies take security at the government center for one day at a time. Sometimes I think we just loved to reinvent the wheel. We wanted things with our stamp on them.

In Ramadi, there was the continual sound of warfare going on. Ramadi was a big city, and the National Guard kept Michigan open and ran patrols, even if they avoided certain areas. We had Marines at Blue Diamond and Hurricane Point, and the National Guard was at Camp Ramadi and Corregidor. We also had COPs around the city. That gave lots of targets for the hajiis to hit. I heard three of the distinctive thunks of outgoing mortars, so I got up to see if I could spot where the rounds would land. I wandered over to where Rick was.

"Any bets on the target?" he asked me.

"The Point?" I hazarded a guess.

"Too close. I think it's us," he replied.

"Maybe," I conceded as I hunched down up against the low wall that surrounded the roof.

"What'd Sylvester want," he asked me.

"Eh, he thinks I should get my FMFEWS qual. Says I would be good at it."

"And here I thought he was a pretty good judge of character. Just goes to show you how wrong you can be," he said.

I reached up to smack him on the back of his helmet just at the mortar landed on the roof. I felt the blast, the heat and dirt flying. At the same time, I felt a sting on the back of my hand and another on my arm. Below us, in the courtyard, I could hear two more explosions, but I was more concerned with my hand. It started to bleed, and I wiped it away to see the damage. It felt worse than it was. I had been hit by one piece of shrapnel in my forearm that looked to have just left a gash, and another small piece was lodged in the back of my hand.

Shouts rang out, checking on everyone. One cut through the cacophony.

"Hey, Doc! Can you come here?"

It was Cpl Choi. He was holding his shin, and I could see the blood staining his cammies. Forgetting my own little scratch, I rushed over. He'd been hit in the front of his leg, which seemed weird. I wasn't sure what he'd been doing to get hit like that.

A machine gun opened up in the distance, and I could hear the rounds chatter as they impacted on the wall of the building. I ducked down as I pulled Cpl Choi's hands away. He'd taken a pretty good gash, and it would need stitches, but like mine, it looked worse than it really was.

Sgt Butler came rushing over. "You OK, John?" he asked.

"Sure thing. Doc's just going to bandage me up, then I'm good to go."

Sgt Butler looked at me, the unspoken question clear. I nodded.

"He's going to be fine," I agreed.

I could put a pressure bandage on him, and then get him taken care of later.

Another huge explosion rocked us, but only smoke made it over the wall. It was probably an RPG, not the most effective weapon while we were in defilade. The mortars undoubtedly fired their load, then took off. Our counterbattery abilities were just too deadly for them to hang around and fire for long.

The squad was returning fire by now, and we had incoming. This was an honest-to-goodness firefight. With all the rounds impacting around us, I knew someone had to get hit just by the law of averages. I could hear the impact of incoming below us, too, in the courtyard and the other buildings.

We had well over a hundred Kilo Company Marines at the compound. There were the other Marines, soldiers, and civilians in the Provincial Reconstruction Team, but they were supposed to hunker down in the event of an attack. And this was a full-fledged attack.

A burst of tracers flew over my head as I ducked down. I wasn't sure how anyone could get direct fire into us on the roof, but those tracers were too close to comfort. The walls on the roof were a good meter high, but I low-crawled to check on each of the Marines. Pierce was hit again, but not seriously. We were here less than two months, and he already had two purple hearts. He had to be some sort of shrapnel magnet. I cleaned out his wound and slapped a bandage on it.

After only a few minutes, the other two squads made it to the roof and everyone shifted to give them room. We had the entire platoon up there. The other two platoons would be down below, keeping any bad guys from coming in. Our job was to support them from our higher vantage point.

A first lieutenant came up the stairs and out onto the roof to join us, his R/O in tow. He had a quick meeting with the lieutenant, then moved to his vantage point. Holding the handset from his radio, his R/O on the ground beside him, he started passing messages.

More tracer rounds went over our heads. The insurgents had to have more than one machine gun targeting us. The arty lieutenant evidently spotted where one of the machine guns was, because he got excited and started giving out coordinates.

The rounds kept pouring in, and an RPG rocket skipped over our heads. I could clearly see it as it crested the wall by about two feet and kept going to land somewhere out there in Indian country.

We could hear the sound when the arty rounds passed over us, on their way from Camp Ramadi to wherever the lieutenant had sent them. For a moment, all of us paused and heads popped up to watch. There were several huge explosions not 400 meters away, and the volume of incoming fire slackened. There were several cheers, and the lieutenant and his R/O gave each other a high five.

Buster Seychik slid up to me and said, "Let me take a look at your hand."

With all that had happened, I had forgotten that I'd been hit. Now that he reminded me, my hand began to burn.

He took a quick look.

"Not much there, but I don't want to remove it here. After all of this is over, we'll get it out. Your arm though, that's a clean cut." He rinsed my hand, bandaged the small hunk of metal in place, then slapped a bandage on my forearm.

The firing slacked off some, but it was pretty constant for the next two hours. We'd been hit before while on patrol, but that was nothing like the sustained attack that was going on. No one on the roof was hit again, but below us, the call of "Corpsman up!" rang out at least three times.

Darkness fell, and that didn't make a difference. We had plenty of night vision goggles, but I couldn't figure that they had any. But that didn't stop them from attacking.

"Man, look at those idiots," I heard Jenner say, looking below with his goggles.

He and Rick raised their weapons when the heavy staccato of a .50 cal opened up.

"Oh, shit!" Rick said in awe. "That fucked up their day!"

"Well, whaddaya expect? Coming across in the open like that. Probably suicide bombers."

"Well, I guess First Platoon only gets a suicide assist on that one, though. Sent them off but good. They should thank First for getting them to their 79 virgins."

I asked Rick to borrow his goggles. I slipped them on, then peeked over the edge of the roof wall.

"Over there, by the northwest corner of the Swiss Cheese," Rick offered helpfully.

I looked in that direction, trying to get my perspective in the flattened, monotone view. It took a moment before what I was seeing registered. There were probably five bodies out there, not 100 meters from the compound. I say probably because two or three of them were so torn up, I couldn't be sure, at this distance, how many parts were there. A .50 cal round would do a lot of damage to a body.

I slid back, then gave the goggles back to Rick. I glanced at my bandaged hand and tried to imagine what would have happened had I been hit by one of the big rounds.

The firing slacked off, then picked up. Slacked off again and picked up. SSgt White said they were firing, then moving. That didn't stop the sniper team on the roof from scoring a couple of kills. There were two teams up there with us: Cpl Lindt, the odd-looking sniper, and his assistant and another team. They seemed to be having some sort of macabre contest to see who could kill the most attackers.

Captain Wilcox came up several times, the last time with another captain. We'd been getting some increased machine gun fire, and along with the first sergeant, 2ndLt Hobbs, and the lieutenant who called in the artillery fire, they discussed this for a few minutes before giving way to the captain who came up with the CO. He had some sort of high-speed-low-drag radio, and he got on it.

"He's the FAO," Cpl Choi said. "They're going to call in air on the bastards."

Five minutes later, the dark became day for an instant as fire erupted skyward about 400 or 500 meters away. An entire building, and anyone inside of it, ceased to exist. It was there one moment, gone the next.

There were exclamations of "Fuck!" and the inevitable "Get some!" At that moment, deep in the very core of my being, I was glad I was an American. Glad I was with the Marines, instead of some third-world insurgent facing them.

The ruins of the building were pretty visible in the resultant fires. Like a campfire, the flames drew and captured the eyes. I think we were offering plenty of targets for a sniper as we watched, but whoever was out there was evidently in no mood to fight. All incoming stopped, except for a single magazine being emptied in our direction about 15 minutes later. I could imagine the frustration and anger one of the attackers must have felt, and emptying the magazine was probably just an expression of that frustration.

After about 30 minutes or so, while still remaining on alert, we began to stand down somewhat. Our platoon had five WIAs, none seriously. First Platoon had two fairly serious WIAs and Third Platoon had one, but despite the huge amount of fire, no one was killed. No Americans, that is. There had to be 20 or 30 Iraqis killed.

HM2 Sylvester checked out my hand again.

"The shrapnel's pretty small, but it's in there tight, and it might be lodged under your tendons. It doesn't make sense to try and pull it out now. I'm going to get you to Charlie Med and let the surgeons take care of it. Don't move your hand anymore, though. If the metal's under one of your tendons or nerves, we don't want you abrading your way through it. You're going to be fine, so don't worry about it."

I never thought that I could actually damage my hand. Could that keep me from become a radiology tech? It was such a tiny piece of metal.

"Here's the hero," Rick said as he came up. "Free license plates for life, right?"

"What?"

"You know, for your Purple Heart. You get free license plates for your car. All for that little bee sting you call a wound. One, I might add, would have been mine if your hand hadn't been in the way."

"Well, sorry I had to save your ass there, Marine. Saved by a squid, huh?"

"Took my benny, more like it. Next time, save some for me. Well, unless it's a big mother fucking grenade or something. In that case, it all yours," he said with a laugh.

"Haddad!" Sgt Butler said as he came up. "You've got the fire team until Cpl Choi's back on full duty. And since Doc Cannon here's going to be on light duty, too, well, I guess you're off the shit burning detail. You two get below, get cleaned up, and get some rest. We're back on in . . ." he paused to look at his watch, "in just about 6 hours."

Chapter 8

Charlie Med, Camp Ramadi
April 27, 2006

"It's your call. We think it will be a fairly simple surgery, but there is a chance of complications. If you'd rather go and get the procedure at Balad, we'll get that done."

The Navy surgeon looked to me for my answer. He had introduced himself to me, but his name slipped my mind, and he didn't have a nametag on his scrubs. I didn't even know his rank.

I looked down at my hand. It was only slightly inflamed, but the little bit of protruding metal was very evident. It was what was under my skin that caused the concern. With the congestion of nerves, bones, and tendons in the hand, taking the piece of shrapnel out could cause more damage than when it went in. Charlie Med had X-ray machines, but not the entire line of diagnostic imaging machines that would let the surgeons know exactly what was happening inside my hand.

For the first time, I began to get a little concerned. I had been told not to flex my fingers, but I involuntarily did so as I looked at my hand. It was a little hard to believe that there was an issue. My hand hurt, but it worked fine. The piece of shrapnel was small, maybe the size of my little fingernail. How could that be causing the surgical team concern when they were used to treating massive injuries?

HM2 Sylvester had been about to tease the shrapnel out of my hand back at the government center, for goodness sake. And now these surgeons hesitated?

I hadn't even been in much of a hurry to seek treatment. I'd caught a ride from the government center late in the morning, then grabbed hot chow at Camp Ramadi first thing. In Ramadi, there was a definite hierarchy of comfort. At the bottom of the ladder was the government center, and probably the COPs. I'm guessing at the COPs as I had never been to one, nor to Corregidor, so I couldn't say for sure from personal experience. Basically speaking, the government center sucked. Next up the ladder was Hurricane Point and Blue Diamond. Most of the Marines were at the Point, and while our SWAs were pretty basic, at least we got hot chow and had a few facilities to make life easier. At the top of the ladder, that

Shangri-la, at least to us Marines, was Camp Ramadi. They had a small PX, or BX, I guess the Army folks called it. Hell, they had organized sports on the base. As I walked to see the docs, I looked on with more than a bit of envy as a team practiced hoops at a makeshift court. I might never have been Kobe Bryant, but I could bring it.

I eventually made my way over to Charlie Med, ready for a quick removal, a stitch or two, then getting back to the Point and my platoon. We were going back on duty in a few hours, and I needed to get back before that. Things weren't working out that way, though. One of the Army docs took a look at my hand, then referred me to the surgical team. I had X-rays taken, then three surgeons took a look while they conferred with each other. This was pretty ridiculous. It was only a tiny piece of shrapnel! Bobo Smith in First Squad had taken a round though-and-through in his biceps during the attack, and he was already back at the Point, arm bandaged up, ready to go out again.

The surgeon was standing there, waiting for my decision. I looked back down at my hand. It really didn't look like much. I didn't understand their concern, to be honest, but I did trust their skill. I'd heard really good things about them, and I'd rather have Navy surgeons than the Air Force surgeons they probably had at Balad. I'm sure the Air Force docs were great and all, but keeping it in the family made sense.

I didn't really want to leave, either. If I went to Balad, when would I get back? Who would take care of my Marines?

That thought struck me. *My Marines?* I just wanted to get done with my tour and move on to C School, right? And now I wanted to get back in time to go on duty? It was a strange world.

I looked back up at the doctor and said, "No, you do it."

A smile broke over his face as he replied, "Great! Let's get you prepped and take care of it!"

One of the nurses helped me off the examining table and led me to a shower, giving me pretty detailed instructions on getting clean. It was overkill, I thought. I knew how to shower, and I was a corpsman, after all. I understood the importance of keeping as sterile an environment as possible.

I got out of the shower and into surgical gown. Like millions of other people who have worn them, I wondered at having my ass hang out in the breeze. There had to be a better way to design them. A different nurse led me to one of the operating tables and had me lay down on it. She was a tiny woman with the dark looks that made

Jonathan P. Brazee

me think she was a Filipina. Tiny or not, she knew how to take charge.

"OK, HA Cannon . . . Zachary, right?" she asked, but went on before I could acknowledge her. "I'm LTJG Quijano. I'll be assisting Dr. Hawkins in this."

Hawkins, LCDR Hawkins. Right! That was the surgeon's name!

"We'll get you sterilized, then we'll give you local. I'm sure there won't be any problems. Dr. Hawkins is about the best there is."

She supervised the attachment of a small, well, tray, I guessed you would call it, on which my arm would be placed, keeping it in a position that gave the surgeon the best access to it. She then told one of the guys, probably a corpsman, but I guessed he could have been a nurse, too, to scrub down my entire arm with a Betadine solution.

Another man came out, probably one of the doctors. It was a bit hard to know who was who when everyone was in scrubs. He spoke with the nurse, then came over to look at my hand.

"This will feel like bee sting," he said in a somewhat rote tone of voice as if he had said it a million times before, "and then it will numb right up."

A "bee sting." That was exactly what I had told that little Iraqi girl before I stitched her up. The tables had turned.

And you know what? It did feel like a bee sting. The first shot, that is. The next two were put into tissue that was already feeling numb.

"You OK, there? How does it feel?" he asked.

"Local analgesia has set in," I answered.

For some reason, I didn't want this doctor to think I was the normal Marine or soldier being brought in, that I was in the medical field myself. So I used "analgesia," sure that no one not in the medical field would use the term. I shouldn't have bothered.

"Good, good," he said. "Let LTJG Quijano know if you begin to feel anything."

He left and the JG moved to my side. She really looked young, younger than me. Younger than Amy. But she was a nurse, so he had to have already earned a nursing degree.

"Dr. Hawkins will be here in a few moments, and we'll get you out of here in no time."

Only he wasn't. Charlie Med got a call about incoming. A National Guard hummer had been hit by an IED. There was one KIA and two WIAs. The surgical team went into hyper drive getting

50

ready for the two wounded soldiers. My entire operating table with me on it was pushed to the side of the room.

The whup-whup of a Black Hawk announced the two soldier's arrival. I could feel the tension in the room increase. I realized this was their war, the medical team, and it was just as important, if not more important, than mine. They might not going out into the fight, but they had their own demons with which to contend. They fought to save life and limb.

The two wounded soldiers were rushed in and placed on the two tables that now took center stage. Charlie Surgical split into two well-oiled machines, one taking each soldier. The soldiers' uniforms were quickly cut off, and they both were swapped down with Betadine. I caught bits and pieces of what was happening as the surgeons shouted out orders.

One soldier was in pretty bad shape. He was the one closest to me, and I saw his uniform was covered in blood as someone shoved the pieces into a plastic bag. His surgeon, LCDR Hawkins ordered blood, and bag after bag was given to him as the team struggled to save him.

I couldn't see as much of the other soldier, but he didn't look as bad off. His team kept focusing on any head wound, noting that his right pupil was dilated and non-responsive. I knew enough, though, to understand that appearances did not always mean who was worse off.

In this case, though, appearances were probably reflective of what was happening. The team on the first soldier got more and more frantic, the tone of the orders being given going up several notches. Dr. Hawkins kept yelling out for more blood as they tried to save the soldier's life. When he reached up from the abdominal cavity and began cardiac compressions, I knew the situation was dire. After ten minutes of that, he slowed, stopped, and stepped back.

"I'm calling it," he said in a subdued voice.

The entire team visibly deflated. In their own war, they had just lost the battle.

Dr. Hawkins seemed to gather himself, then moved over to the other table, careful not to get too close and contaminate that theater. He asked for an update.

I kept staring at the dead soldier as two people in scrubs started cleaning up the scene, so I didn't catch everything. Essentially, the second soldier had some minor and moderate injuries that had been taken care of, but he was concussed and needed care. Dr. Hawkins ordered a medevac, then left the room.

Jonathan P. Brazee

"We need to change and get scrubbed, but we'll be back for you," LTJG Quijano said as she approached me.

I looked over at my hand again. One tiny piece of shrapnel, one little speck of iron. That was nothing. Over on that other table, not five meters from me, a soldier lay dead. I felt like an imposter, a malingerer.

I just nodded and continued to watch as the soldier's body was given the first steps necessary to get him back home to his family. When the black plastic body bag came out, there was a degree of finality to it.

They used a body bag on the other soldier, too. Iraq is a hot place, of course. But when flying wounded, the docs wanted to keep the patients warm, and the body bags did a pretty good job at that. We called them "hot pockets."

The dead soldier's body was taken out to the temporary morgue while a soldier consulted with some of Charlie Surgical's staff about the casevac. I overheard the name of the wounded soldier: Specialist 4 Ernesto Padilla Pérez. While they were getting ready to bring him outside to meet the incoming Black Hawk, he began to stir for the first time. One of the team members put his hand on the body bag where is covered the soldier's leg, obviously trying to give comfort. It had the opposite effect. I think Spec 4 Padilla Pérez must have come to and realized he was in a body bag and thought he had died. He started shouting about being dead, and it took several minutes and four people to calm him down, to assure him he was alive and going to get help. Whether they got through or not, or whether the half-conscious soldier simply drifted back into full unconsciousness, I wasn't sure.

Right about then, Dr. Hawkins and his team came back in. It was like they all were different people. They had left dejected, and they came back seemingly ready to go. I was moved back over to center stage, right in the same spot that the first soldier had died.

"HA Cannon, you ready to get your hand taken care of?" he asked, pulling up my chart once more.

"Yes, sir," I answered.

I just wanted to get out of Charlie Surgical and back to my squad.

The doctor had me re-sterilized, and I was given the anesthetic again as the first series had already worn off. Surrounded by the team, the doctor began to explore my hand.

On my back, the surgical lights were extremely bright, almost painfully bright. I guessed most of their patients were unconscious, so maybe it didn't matter.

52

"Well, that was easy," I heard him say.

I looked over to see Dr. Hawkins hold aloft a small piece of shrapnel in his forceps. It was already out.

"Let's take a look here and see what damage was done," he said.

I didn't think he was talking to me, so I didn't respond.

He poked around my hand for a few minutes, asking the opinions of some of the others before he stepped back.

"Nothing. No damage."

He picked the forceps back up and held them in front of me. I could see two very jagged edges, sort of protrusions that had been under my skin.

"You're a lucky man, there, Cannon. If anyone had tried to simply pull this up and out of your hand, you would have needed microsurgery to make the repairs. Even then, your hand may never have been back to 100%. But coming back exactly on the path it took in, well, it came out without a whimper. Your hand is fine."

Yesterday, I would have said my hand would be fine. But with all the concern expressed since then, my anxiety level had risen. It was a huge relief to hear the surgeon's words.

"We're going to flush this out, then give you a couple of sutures and send you back to your unit."

I felt a squeeze on my other arm. I looked over to see LTJG Quijano. Even with her mask covering her face, I could see from her eyes that she was smiling.

Her smile, however, could not possibly be bigger than the one that took over my face as I heard the news.

Chapter 9

Ramadi
April 28, 2006

Another house call. I wasn't sure what mission I dislike the most. At the Government House, we were essentially targets, waiting for the bad guys to come. But we were in back of walls or up on the roof, and we had fire support dialed in. In a house call, we were skulking around in the middle of the night, out there in the bad guys' neighborhoods. We were moving on our terms, taking the fight to them, but we were way more exposed.

A house call was when we were given the names and location of a bomb maker, leader of the insurgency, or any high-level target. We'd go out in the middle of the night and try and take the guy—alive if possible, but dead was OK, too. On a normal patrol we didn't have a specific target, so we could go as the skipper, the lieutenant, or as Sgt Butler deemed fit. On a house call, however, we needed to get the guy.

This was a platoon operation. First and Second had their own targets, and the skipper wanted all three "served" at the same time. Other than the timing, though, we were on our own.

We were already in the small alley near our target, just waiting for the other two platoons to get into their positions. This time, Second Squad would be the first to bust inside the house. Third Squad was positioned in another small alley in back of the house, and First Squad would provide additional security towards the front of the target building and reinforce us if needed.

I looked down at my hand. It was dark, and I had a glove on, so I couldn't see anything. I'd take a bit of good-natured shit from the others on it. It certainly looked less serious than most of what the other wounded Marines had. I didn't bother to tell them that another millimeter more or someone casually taking it out would have resulted in permanent damage. I just nodded, said I was a pussy, and let it go. Without me fighting back, it wasn't any fun, and it was soon forgotten. HM2 Sylvester was the only one I told. I figured he should know that his decision not to try and remove it was the right one.

We waited in the dark for close to 30 minutes. The longer we waited, the more exposed we were. As a rule, Iraqis in Ramadi didn't get out and about at night too much. But that is not to say no one did. The guys setting the IEDs sure did. Other people did, too, when they had to get something done. We didn't need some passerby to stumble on us crouching in the dark and then raise the alarm.

Finally, the lieutenant must have gotten the word because he motioned Sgt Butler to move out. Carefully, hugging the walls of the buildings alongside the alley, we moved our stack forward. We got to the road, and right across the street from us was our target, a non-descript, two-story building. Like most homes in Ramadi that didn't front right on the street, this one had a masonry wall in front of it, the metal gate opening out onto the street. In back of the wall would be a smallish courtyard, then the house itself another six or seven meters back.

Sgt Butler flipped down his night vision goggles, moved forward, and looked down the road on both sides. It must have been clear because he sent Cpl Dunlop and his team rushing over and up against the home's wall as the assault element. Cy Pierce reached up and slowly tried to pull the gate latch open.

Usually, these latches were locked. Sometimes, they were not locked, but opening them made a loud enough screech to raise the dead. This time, we were lucky. The latch opened, and Second Fire Team slipped inside. A few long moments later, a hand stuck back out the gate and motioned us forward.

Rick's Third Fire Team, which was the support element, rushed forward along with Sgt Butler and me. We slipped inside the gate and into a courtyard. The use of cement made it fairly light inside, and visibility was pretty good for 2:30 in the morning. There was nothing too remarkable about it, no big surprises. It was about 6 meters deep and ran the length of the house. Halfway to the house was a small step, then a two concrete pillars held up a small roof covering the front doors. Cpl Dunlop had his two Marines up against the building just to the left of the door. Rick took his two Marines and moved up to the building to the right of the door.

As Sgt Butler and I stopped by the courtyard's step, what looked liked a large flowerpot gave a whump and fell apart. That's what it looked like to me, at least. Granted, it was dark, but I was looking right at it when the front seemed to fall off and to the hard deck of the courtyard. We heard a shout from the second story, but it didn't seem to register to me.

It did to Sgt Butler. He grabbed me and literally threw me up against the house as the world erupted into noise. Small arms fire started pouring out from all three second story windows. Rounds

Jonathan P. Brazee

started pinging around the courtyard, throwing up chips of cement. I looked back at the dust that was rising from where I had been standing just a moment before. If Sgt Butler hadn't reacted like he did, I would already have been dead meat. This close to the wall, those above were having a hard time hitting us, but the rounds that were striking only a foot from us were proof that if we weren't up against the wall, we would be getting clobbered.

I hugged the front of the house as fire from First Squad began to impact above us. The Marines with me swiveled up and began to fire, trying to keep whomever was up there from firing down at us.

Steve Jenner was laying just to my right. He pulled out a grenade, shouted "Frag," and looked to try and loft it in one of the windows above me. Rick lunged forward to grab his hand.

"The angle's too shallow!" he shouted. "It'll fall back down on us!"

The Iraqis above us didn't have the same problem. A grenade came flying down, but the thrower hadn't gotten a good enough angle, so it bounced away a couple of meters, towards the front of the courtyard. Several voices yelled out "Grenade!" as we all tried to burrow into the concrete. The explosion was huge, but no one was hit.

Lying there in the ground, I looked over to the flower pot that had fallen apart. From this vantage, I could see a wire coming out of the back of it. It had been rigged to explode, but for the grace of God, something had gone wrong. The thing had only partially detonated. And that was why I was still alive. That and Sgt Butler pulling me out of the kill zone.

A strong arm grabbed the back of my flak jacket and pulled my face off the deck.

"Fire your fucking weapon, Doc!" Sgt Butler screamed at me.

I looked at him in confusion. I was the corpsman, not one of them. I hadn't fired my weapon since FMSS back at Pendleton.

"Now, Doc!" he thundered.

I was clutching my M16 in my hands, and I looked down on it for a moment. I turned to my back, raised the muzzle and pulled the trigger. Nothing happened. I pulled the rifle back down to look at it before I remembered the safety. I flipped it off, then raised the weapon, pulling the trigger. The soft kick barely registered as I put several rounds up into the air. I honestly could not see where I was aiming or if I was hitting anything. Rounds were impacting all over the wall, sending dust and bits of cement raining down on us. I stopped and pulled out my goggles, putting them on to protect my eyes. I raised my weapon again and fired.

56

"Everyone! Face down and cover!" shouted the squad leader. He said something over the small PRR, then a few moments later, it seemed like half of the wall on the second floor was taken out with a huge explosion. Debris fell around us. One of the attached SMAW gunners from Weapons Platoon had evidently done his thing.

We spun back around and began to fire again, but it was evident that the firing from above had stopped. We heard shouting in Arabic from inside as people ran to get away. And they did get away out the back, until Third Squad opened up, that is. We could hear a pretty fierce firefight, but it was short. In less than a minute, firing ceased.

I got up to check the Marines. A piece of wall had fallen on La'Ron, maybe breaking a few fingers, but amazingly, that was about it. Seven Marines and one sailor had been in the kill zone, and not one of us had been hit by enemy fire. It would have been a different story, though, if that first booby trap had detonated. We might of all been killed given the confined nature of the courtyard.

Then it hit me. They knew we were coming. The open gate, the booby trap, the insurgents ready to fire. This whole things had been a set up. If this was a set up, then the other two platoons had probably been set up as well.

Set up or not, we cleared the building. On the second floor, we found two dead insurgents, blown apart by the SMAW. Several blood trails proved that some of them had been hit but were still alive to try and make their escape.

When we linked up with Third Squad, they had three more insurgents, two dead, and one being treated by Buster Seychik. From the amount of fire that had been pouring down on us, it seemed hard to believe that there had only been five of them.

The platoon had been pretty lucky, even if Marines like Sgt Butler had made some of that luck themselves. I knew I was alive because of him, and maybe some of the others were as well.

Third Platoon had not been so lucky. While First Platoon had gone into an empty target, Third had gone into the same type of ambush as we had. They killed two insurgents, but had two KIAs and three serous WIAs. One of the KIAs was HM Sean Gruber, USN.

Chapter 10

Hurricane Point
April 29, 2006

"Did you know him well?" Rick asked.

That was a good question. Of course I knew him—him being HM Gruber. When Senior Chief called a meeting of the battalion's corpsmen or when we had training, he was there, too. And when all the corpsmen and our families had that pre-deployment dinner at the Golden Corral, he and I had talked. But knew him well? He and I might have been junior corpsmen, we might have both been US Navy, but I knew the Marines in my squad much better.

"I knew him, yea. We weren't bosom buddies, but yea, I knew him," was all I finally came up with.

"Well, yea," was Rick's short comment.

"That sucks," he added after a few moments.

Rick and I were the only ones in our hootch at the moment. The other Marines were probably still at chow. We sat down on facing bunks, not really knowing what to say. We'd already lost one Marine KIA and another WIA and medevac'd back to the States, but dealing with death was something that we all had to come to grips with.

On one hand, for me, at least, there was a bit of a relief, guilty relief that is wasn't me, that it wasn't Rick or one of the others in the squad. That was a pretty messed up emotion, I know. Sean had his own friends, his own family back home, and to them, his death occupied center stage. The feeling of relief I felt made no sense, anyway. It was not like there was a quota on deaths, that if someone else bought it, that would somehow make our odds any better. If anything, it made the odds worse, what with fewer people taking the fight to the enemy.

The hatch opened and in walked Sgt Butler.

"Can you give us a moment there, Haddad?" he asked as he stood there.

I had been somewhat avoiding him after his blowup at me during the fight. I admired the man, and I had not been particularly happy that I had not met his expectations.

He stood silently as Rick gathered his gear and left. As the hatch closed behind Rick, he pulled out a piece of paper and handed it to me. I took it and looked. It was a copy of a photo, obviously pulled from the internet and printed out.

The subject was a statue. The base of the statue was large, maybe ten feet long and five feet high, made up of stones mortared in place and with a plaque affixed to the side. There were two figures on top, both WWII-era military. One was lying on his back. At his head crouched another figure, one hand holding what looked to be a plasma bag, another holding outstretched a .45.

"Do you know what that is?" he asked me.

"A statue of a corpsman, or maybe an Army medic," I answered.

"But of who?"

Something tweaked in the back of my mind, but I wasn't making the connection.

"Um, . . . I'm not sure."

"The hospital at the Stumps?" he prodded.

"Oh, is that Robert Bush?" I asked.

The hospital at 29 Palms was named after Robert Bush, a corpsman who had been awarded the Medal of Honor back in WWII. We had been told about him back at school. He'd been wounded, refused evacuation, and treated his Marines all the while fighting the Japanese soldiers.

He handed me another piece of paper. On it was the citation for Bush's Medal.

"I want you to read that," he told me.

I looked back down and began to read:

CITATION:

Rank and organization: Hospital Apprentice First Class, U.S. Naval Reserve, serving as Medical Corpsman with a rifle company, 2d Battalion, 5th Marines, 1st Marine Division.

Place and date: Okinawa Jima, Ryukyu Islands, 2 May 1945.

Entered service at: Washington.

Born: 4 October 1926, Tacoma, Wash.

Citation: For conspicuous gallantry and intrepidity at the risk of his life above and beyond the call of duty while serving as Medical

Jonathan P. Brazee

Corpsman with a rifle company, in action against enemy Japanese forces on Okinawa Jima, Ryukyu Islands, 2 May 1945. Fearlessly braving the fury of artillery, mortar, and machinegun fire from strongly entrenched hostile positions, Bush constantly and unhesitatingly moved from 1 casualty to another to attend the wounded falling under the enemy's murderous barrages. As the attack passed over a ridge top, Bush was advancing to administer blood plasma to a marine officer lying wounded on the skyline when the Japanese launched a savage counterattack. In this perilously exposed position, he resolutely maintained the flow of life-giving plasma. With the bottle held high in 1 hand, Bush drew his pistol with the other and fired into the enemy's ranks until his ammunition was expended. Quickly seizing a discarded carbine, he trained his fire on the Japanese charging pointblank over the hill, accounting for 6 of the enemy despite his own serious wounds and the loss of 1 eye suffered during his desperate battle in defense of the helpless man. With the hostile force finally routed, he calmly disregarded his own critical condition to complete his mission, valiantly refusing medical treatment for himself until his officer patient had been evacuated, and collapsing only after attempting to walk to the battle aid station. His daring initiative, great personal valor, and heroic spirit of self-sacrifice in service of others reflect great credit upon Bush and enhance the finest traditions of the U.S. Naval Service.

I finished reading and looked back up at the still-standing squad leader.

"Zach," he began, "you are a good corpsman, and people have noticed. You're pretty green, but you don't lack balls. And you care. Everyone in the squad's happy with you as our doc."

I didn't like the direction that this was going. It sounded like a breakup—*you are a great guy and all, and any girl would be happy to have you , but . . .* —and the thought of that was surprisingly painful. Not all corpsmen were suited to going out with the Marines. Some just couldn't hack it, and those corpsmen were quietly transferred back to the aid station or one of the hospitals.

That is what I really wanted—to be in a hospital, right? So why was I feeling a sense of dread coming over me?

"What I want to point out is that you are supposed to be a Fleet Marine Force corpsman, a combat corpsman. You seem to be forgetting that. You get trained to shoot; we give you an M16 and a full combat load. Why do that unless you are supposed to fight?

60

"Right now, we are short-handed. We need every swinging dick to get into the mix. Last night, we were pretty much in a shit sandwich, and there you were hugging the concrete. I needed you to put some rounds downrange."

I understood what he was saying, but I never really thought of my job as fighting. That was for the Marines in the squad. I was just there to patch them up if they got hit. I put down the citation and picked up the picture of the statue again. Well, Robert Bush hadn't idly stood by, waiting for a patient. He treated with one hand, killed Japs with another.

"Have you heard of the Order of St. John?" he asked me.

I shook my head no.

"Their full name is The Sovereign Hospitaller Order of St John of Jerusalem, of Rhodes, and of Malta, now usually just referred to as the Knights of Malta."

He waited for me to acknowledge that, but I stared back up at him blankly.

"The Knights of Malta, from the Crusades?" he asked as he sat down on the bunk opposite me.

"Yea, I know the Crusades."

"And do you know what the Order of St. John did?"

"Well, they fought the Muslims, right? To get back the Holy Land?"

He sighed and said, "Well, sort of. They did fight. But what was their mission? Think of what's in their name. *Hospitaller*."

Something clicked. "They were doctors?"

"Not quite," he said, "but you made the connection to where we got the word 'hospital.' But no, they weren't doctors. They were medieval versions of medical assistants. They were founded about a thousand years ago to serve sick and wounded crusaders and pilgrims, helping the doctors and doing all the care, you know, like changing bandages, feeding, cleaning up, lancing boils and whatnot, all that medical stuff. In other words, they were the world's first corpsmen."

All of that was well and good, but I wondered where he was going with it all. As long as I didn't hear that I was fired, though, anything else he had to say was welcomed, and he seemed to be on a roll.

"They were the first chivalrous order, and from them, we get all our ideas of how knights are supposed to act. They also took vows of poverty and chastity, though, and to serve the Pope. What they didn't do was take vows of non-violence. Quite the contrary, they were perhaps the fiercest warriors of the Crusades.

"When Suleiman the Magnificent attacked the fortress on Rhodes, the home of the knights, he attacked with over 200,000 men. The knights were only about 500 men. But they held out for six months, beating back every Ottoman attack. What got them was when they ran out of food. Starving, they surrendered, and Suleiman let them keep their arms and sail away in recognition of their courage and tenacity.

"The reason I'm telling you all of this is because I want to show you that the first corpsmen, the first medics, so to speak, were maybe healers first, but they were still warriors. And that's what you need to be, a warrior.

"Look, no one doubts your balls. If we did, you'd be gone. But you need to get it in your head that you're a 'combat corpsman,' and that you are not just an observer of the fight, you are part of it."

He paused to let me take it all in. I had no problem with the fighting. It wasn't like I was a conscientious objector. I just don't think I ever got it into my mindset. My rifle was for personal protection, like 2ndLt Hobbs carried a weapon, like Capt Wilcox, hell, like the colonel carried one. But what he said made sense.

I still wanted to be a radiology tech. I needed a career after all of this, a way to support my family. But I was with the Marines now, and I was going to do my best with them, not just because I needed a good recommendation for C School, but because I liked them all and felt the *esprit de corps* the Marines always gave homage to. I felt part of them all.

I looked back at the picture of Robert Bush's statue. He'd made his choice. I figured the Knights of Malta would have been mighty proud of him.

"So whaddaya think," Sgt Butler asked me. "You onboard?"

I shrugged my acceptance. "A vow of poverty's no problem. I'm just getting E2 pay, anyway. But do I have to give a vow of chastity?"

Chapter 11

Ramadi
May 4, 2006

"Holy shit!" Jarod muttered.

I seconded the feeling. We had gone out on patrol in the bright sunlight, and now the sun was blocked. Up ahead, we could see an immense cloud of sand rolling our way.

Things had changed over the last few days. The National Guard was getting ready to go back home, and the Army was sending a mechanized brigade in to take their place, the "Ready First," they called themselves. This was a much bigger force. Where the 2/28 BCT had five tanks, I think, the Ready First had 40 or 50. We'd already gotten the word that we, and that included the Marines, were going to be more aggressive in taking it to the enemy.

I never really understood why we were under the National Guard, and now the Army, as soon as they officially took command, when they in turn answered to I MEF back at Fallujah. Our big boss was a Marine, then the next was Army, then we got to the battalion. And even us, we were a Camp Lejeune battalion, but we were under a Camp Pendleton MEF. Then again, all of that was above my pay grade—way above it.

What we all did know, even us peons, was that Ramadi was heating up. Some people said we were losing the city. Others said we had to go and Fallujah it, just move in and take out the bad guys. What that ignored was that most of our bad guys had been in Fallujah and had been driven out, taking up residence in Ramadi. If we did the same thing here, they'd just go to Haditha or some such place.

While the colonels and generals hashed out what we would do, those of us on the pointy end of the spear hoped they'd get it right. Not that they'd ask us, of course. We'd just do what they ordered us to do, and if they were wrong, we'd pay the price.

This patrol was one of those we hated. We had no specific target. We were just out, being seen, and becoming a target. We would be moving north to the High Water Bridge that provided one of the avenues into the city, then come back. It was routine, but still stressful.

Jonathan P. Brazee

It was routine until the mother of all sand storms kicked up, that is. It looked just like the storm in *The Mummy*, coming down to engulf us. Sgt Butler got on the hook with the lieutenant, but the word came to continue with the mission.

This was a platoon patrol. Each of the three squads was advancing up its own route—each route being an adjacent street. We needed to advance at the same rate so we could support each other if need be. This storm would wreck havoc with that.

The day turned to a dark, orangish dusk as the huge dust cloud rose above us. We could almost smell the ozone in the air. The streets of Ramadi were always pretty empty, but now the place was a ghost town. Doors and windows were tightly shut.

When the storm hit us, it hit us like a fist. I literally staggered. If I didn't have my goggles on, I would have been blinded. Even with the goggles, I could barely see my hand in front of my face.

Tactical dispersion eroded away as I think all of us feared getting separated from each other. We closed it up until we could see the outlines of those directly in front and in back of us. We gravitated towards the buildings to the right, not so much as a guide to keep us moving, but hoping that the walls would offer even a bit of protection.

I pulled up the kerchief higher on my face. I was pretty well covered, but the sand was stinging me where it struck my cheeks and nose.

We slowly moved forward. I couldn't see him, but I figured Sgt Butler was keeping tabs on the rest of the platoon. I really thought it would be better if we hunkered down until the storm blew itself out, but we'd been briefed that some storms could last for a couple of days.

I ran up the back of Jarod, who'd stopped dead in his tracks. Looking around him, we had run up into Third Fire Team. I could barely make out the bulky figure of Cpl Choi, back now on full duty. The Marines seemed to be looking at something ahead.

Cpl Mays passed me to join the others, then with hand and arm signals, we started to get online, spreading out across the street. I still couldn't see what was up. It wasn't until I got abreast of the others that I could barely make out two figures crouching in the street, busy at some task.

We didn't need much stealth with the sand storm giving us cover, but we moved forward, the flanks of our impromptu line bending around to circle the two men. I kept expecting them to jump up and run, but then I realized that while our viz was crap, I could see the two men didn't have goggles. They were trying to protect their eyes with cloth, and with us surrounding them, that was far from effective.

What they were doing became pretty clear. They were digging a hole in the road, ready to emplace an IED. Normally, they did this kind of thing at night, but they must have thought the stand storm would give them cover. That made some sense. They wouldn't be seen by aircraft, which was all grounded. But that didn't take into account a foot patrol.

It was sort of surreal. We had most of the squad surrounding the two guys, but they didn't notice us. Should we just take them out? Should we go up and make introductions?

I couldn't tell of sure, but it looked like it was Cpl Choi who stepped close, then poked one of the men in the back with his weapon. The guy jumped up, knocking over the one who was doing the digging.

My finger tensed on the trigger. I hadn't had a real target since Sgt Butler's talk a few days before. I'd at least return fire the day before when we'd taken fire, but I really hadn't seen who I was shooting at. This time, they were right in front of me. Of course, there were other members of the squad in front of me, too. When I realized that, I had a gut check. I hoped whoever was in back of me realized I was in front of him.

The two men jumped up, then froze, hands in the air. It didn't look like they'd be fighting. Marines moved forward to flex-cuff their hands behind them and move them to the side of the road and up against a wall.

The initial brunt of the sand storm lessened a bit. Viz still sucked, but instead of five feet, it was probably 15 feet. I got my first look at the insurgents. They were pretty well wrapped up, but one of them looked young, maybe 15 or 16 years old. The other guy was an oldster.

Sgt Butler reported the capture, and we were told to wait there. The lieutenant was on his way. We set up a hasty defensive perimeter with the captives in the middle.

It took the platoon commander almost 15 minutes to make it the one block to us, which seemed like an awful long time, sandstorm or no. He was with Third Squad who did a sort of passage of lines with us to provide flank security. He probably moved First Squad in so we were now in the center.

The lieutenant, SSgt White, and Champ Dykstra, the comm section R/O, moved up to the Iraqis, our interpreter in tow.

Azar was the translator normally assigned to us. He was Iraqi, an Arab, but he was a Christian. He seemed pretty happy to be working for us, and we thought it was not just for the pay, which was pretty good by Iraqi standards. He sometimes ate lunch with us, and he was a bloodthirsty little bastard. He seemed to relish the idea of taking it to his Muslim countrymen.

"Warrior doc" or not, being a corpsman still had some bennies, so I sidled up closer to the prisoners so I could hear what was going on.

Azar was puffing up his chest and yelling in the faces of the now cowering men. I have no idea what he was telling them, but probably that we were going to cut off their heads or wrap them in pig skins before burying them in unconsecrated soil. Azar had told us quite often that he threatened prisoners to "loosen their tongues" and that he enjoyed seeing them squirm.

The lieutenant was used to Azar's little games, so he gave him a few minutes before he started asking questions. I was surprised, though, at how easily the two prisoners spilled. They both readily admitted that they were laying an IED (rather hard to deny considering we caught them in the act.) They said they had been forced by some "foreigners" to plant the explosive, and that they would be killed if they didn't. How that jived with the fact that they had been promised $500 as well, I wasn't sure.

They kept bouncing back and forth between asking both Allah and the lieutenant for forgiveness and begging for their lives. The young kid seemed to have a rather stoic expression on his face, but the old guy was shitting bricks. He was flat out scared.

The lieutenant asked the company for instructions, and about ten minutes later, we were told to hang tight. Battalion wanted to send out an EOD team to blow the IED in place, and we couldn't leave it unattended. Capt Wilcox didn't want us to split the platoon to bring back the prisoners, so we would just sit there until the EOD team came and did their thing.

That actually took less time than normal. Two Bradleys made their way to us, and out came the Guardsmen. They rigged the IED, sending out a small robot to lay some C4 on it, and with us moved way back, blew it in place. Even with the storm still raging, the explosion was epic.

We bundled the two prisoners into one of the Bradleys. That was probably going to piss off battalion. The Bradleys would be going back to Camp Ramadi, not Hurricane Point, so we were passing them out of Marine hands. On paper, at least, it might look like it was the Guard who made the capture, not us. Some officer promotions probably relied on less than that.

Even in war, even with brother Americans, politics sometimes raised its ugly head.

Chapter 12

The Government Center
May 16, 2006

At 8:20 local, 16 May 2006, Sergeant Derek Butler, USMC, Second Squad, Second Platoon, Kilo Company, Third Battalion, Eighth Marines, was shot and killed at the Government Center, Ramadi, Al Anbar, Iraq.

His battle gear was on and fastened as he made his way from the main building to our berthing when out of the blue, a single sniper round hit him at the base of his neck, right above the top of his flak jacket. The round entered just below his Adam's Apple and crushed at least two of his cervical vertebrae. He was dead before his body hit the ground.

I was about ten meters in back of him when he fell. One look told me he was gone, but I started CPR anyway, refusing to acknowledge it. I kept it up until we got him back to battalion.

I cried when LT Henry, the battalion surgeon, told me to stop.

Chapter 13

Ramadi
May 31, 2006

Cpl Mays gave the order to move out. It felt good to be back in a vehicle. The hummers couldn't protect against everything, but they felt safer to me.

We were escorting an Air Force colonel from Baghdad and his team to go meet the governor. I didn't really know what the meeting was about, nor did I really care too much. Another convoy had made it down Michigan not even 20 minutes ago, so the way was likely clear.

My attitude had changed quite a bit since Sgt Butler had been killed. Now, when we went out, I half-way hoped that someone would try to hit us. That would give us the opportunity to hit back, hit back hard. I thought most of the squad felt the same.

Cpl Mays had taken over the squad. At first, SSgt White told us that one of the sergeants from Weapons would take over, but the ten of us asked the lieutenant to back Mays. He took care of it.

Rick, as the senior lance corporal, took over First Fire Team. He was up to strength, but the other two teams were down to three Marines. When we went out, I started slipping into Third Team, giving them an extra body.

While I supported Cpl Mays taking over the squad, now I was having second thoughts. I thought he had been the strongest fire team leader, but he was not Sgt Butler. I just didn't feel as comfortable with him in charge, and I'd already had one argument with him over some piddly-ass shit.

I was riding shotgun with LCpl Whitten as our driver, the same Whitten from H & S, I'd gotten into that fight with back at the Point with Rick. That was all behind us, and we were actually on pretty good terms now. La'Ron had the .50 cal. In the back, we had two civilians, a middle-aged man and a youngish woman. The man had quite a potbelly on him, and his black flak jacket was bursting at the seams to try and contain it. His face was red, whether from the heat, exertion, or if that was his normal color, I couldn't tell. He did not seem to be happy to have left the comfort of the Green Zone to go out gallivanting around in Ramadi.

Welcome to my world, I thought.

The woman was a different story. She had that sort of gaunt look that some ultra-marathoners had. Her flak and helmet seemed more natural on her, and she shook my hand with a sense of purpose, as if trying to show how tough she was. Both of them had given me their names, but frankly, I had forgotten them as soon as I was told.

Ramadi in June was brutally hot, and keeping on all our gear took a strong sense of discipline. Having seen some of the burn cases, though, helped keep the focus on why we wore them.

Knowing why, though, was not the same as meekly accepting it. I realized I was a little tightly-strung after Sgt Butler was killed. I got a little angrier more easily. Besides my argument with Mays, I'd even gotten into an argument with Amy the other day when we spoke on the phone. So if I picked at the edge of my gloves, unraveling the seam, well, better they take the brunt of my mood than a person.

We made pretty good time going down Michigan. I caught faces and a few bodies as we passed, but no one seemed too interested in them.

"Hey, hand my up a water," La'Ron asked.

One thing about Iraq, out in the middle of the desert, we had plenty of water. We had bottles of it everywhere. I'd started reading some history after my talk with Sgt Butler, about the Knights of the Order of St. John and the Crusades, and they'd had no ready source of water in their war. More than a few men had died of thirst while marching over the hot desert sands. In the First Crusade, two thirds of the force died before reaching Jerusalem, a good portion of them dying from hunger, thirst, and disease.

I handed up the bottle, placing it into La'Ron's questing hand, sort of like handing off a baton in a relay race. He wasn't about to take his eyes off the road just to get the bottle.

We drove for another two or three minutes when La'Ron called out that there was trouble ahead, just at the radio sounded, telling us to halt.

"What's going on?" I asked La'Ron, not able to see anything.

"It looks like we've got some big-ass truck stuck up there, trying to get turned around," he called down through the turret.

Anything out of the ordinary was reason for concern, and once during our workups at the Stumps, the aggressor force had used a flatbed to stop us before hitting us from the flanks. I started scanning to the side, checking out each doorway and window.

"What's up, son?" the quavering voice of our passenger reached out.

I didn't know if he was asking me or Whitten, but I answered, "Nothing to worry about. I'll tell you if you need to know anything."

I knew we were supposed to call civilians "sir" and all of that. He was probably some civilian big-wig, and he probably had afternoon tea or whatever with half the generals in the country. But I wasn't in the mood to pacify the guy. Let him report me if he wanted.

We listened to the radio chatter as Cpl Mays reported back to the platoon, asking for instructions. The debate seemed to be on whether the truck could get out of the way on its own, if we needed an Army wrecker to come pull it out, or if we should re-route down one of the uncleared roads.

Our hummer had air-conditioning, but on this one, the air worked better when we were cruising. Sitting there, it struggled to keep us cool. The woman was OK with it, not complaining, but the guy asked us several times if we could turn it up, like this was some limo back in the States. His whining was getting to me.

"Jeeze, can you just shut up?" I finally broke, opening the door to the hummer and stepping out.

I stood there for a moment, trying to look ahead to see the truck for myself. I just couldn't take it anymore. I don't know what was worse—this whining fat fuck, being stuck in back of a damn truck, Cpl Mays screwing up—I wasn't sure. But I couldn't just sit there.

I had been standing there for half a minute or so, taking deep breaths, trying to calm down, when I was kicked high up on my chest by a mule. I went down to my knees, unable to breathe. I heard my weapon clatter to the dust, and I blindly groped to get it back.

I was vaguely aware of the .50 cal opening up above my head, of shouting. I was more concerned with breathing. The thought struck me that I was drowning out in the middle of the friggin' desert, and despite everything, that made me laugh. And when I laughed, I realized I was breathing again. That brought everything back into focus.

I reached up to my chest, feeling for damage. There was no blood, but my chest hurt like a son-of-a-bitch. I opened my flak jacket, and there was no blood inside either. I gingerly touched my chest, and that hurt even more. I probably needed to see if any ribs were broken, but that would have to wait a bit.

La'Ron had stopped firing, the cascade of spent brass littering around me. The hummer in front of us, the one with Rick in it, had gotten into the fight as well, turning towards the right. Jarod fired a few more bursts, and it was only then that I saw the target. Just off to the right was a van, or what was left of it. It had been parked in one of the small side alleys, the side of it facing us. The sliding side door was open just a hair. The .50 cal rounds had pretty much made mincemeat of the van—it wasn't going to go anywhere under its own power.

There was shouting up ahead, and from my vantage point sitting on the ground, I could see Marines pulling the truck driver out and onto the ground. He was screaming something as they threw him face first into the dirt, pulling his hand and zip-tying them in back of his head.

From the other hummers, Marines piled out and advanced to the van. I heard La'Ron swivel the .50, and I looked up to see his back. Good man. He was now covering our rear, giving no one the chance to use the commotion to come up on us that way.

The Marines in the squad bounded up, covering each other. Rob Runolfson was the first one to reach it. He gave the door a push before stepping back. When nothing happened, he looked in again. Immediately he stood up straight and motioned the others to come forward.

Rick looked in, then turned around and shouted "Corpsman up!"

I was still sitting when he had shouted that out. Almost by instinct, I started to get to my feet.

"Zach, get up here!" he shouted again, his hand motioning me forward.

I lurched forward, ignoring the calls from the civilian inside the hummer. When I reached the van, only 10 or 15 meters away, Rick seemed to notice that I wasn't moving right.

"You OK, Zach?"

I realized that he didn't know I'd been shot. He'd just reacted to La'Ron opening up.

"I'm fine," I said. "What do you got?"

I peered inside the van. There were two men there. One, his hand still clutched through the hand strap of a camcorder, was very dead. He'd been hit at least four times, the big .50 cal rounds tearing him apart. The inside of the van looked like a slaughterhouse his blood and flesh dripping everywhere. The heavy smell of shit was almost overpowering, like a physical assault.

The second man, though, was still alive. He looked up at me, his surprisingly green eyes pleading for help. He'd been hit twice, it looked like, once in the arm and another in the back of the shoulder.

I started to move forward when Rick stopped me, telling Rob to disarm the man. It was only then that I saw the rifle beneath him.

Things clicked. This was the guy who had shot me.

I had a brief flash where I wanted to step up and kick the shit out of him. I could have been killed! But then, my training kicked in. Enemy or not, I needed to see what I could do.

I checked him first, running my hands over him, to see where he'd been hit. For all swiss cheese the two .50 cals had made this van into, for all that they had completely torn apart his companion, it was amazing that he had been hit only twice. His left arm was pretty bad, and I doubted the doctors could save it, but while the shot in the shoulder had obviously broken the scapula, that bone had been enough to slightly deflect the big round, sending it running down the back before exiting, then creasing his buttock. It caused a lot of damage, but it never penetrated enough to hit any vital organs.

I left the back alone and addressed the arm. The humerus was splintered into tiny fragments, and the lower arm was hanging on by only a few threads of flesh and tendons. I turned him over, eliciting a grunt as his back wound touched the floor of the van.

Yea, how do you like them apples, you bastard? I couldn't help think for a moment before I forced my corpsman face back on.

I put a tourniquet on his upper arm, then brought the mangled remains over his stomach. As I was bandaging them into place, SSgt White, who was with us on the mission, came up.

"What's the status here, Doc?"

I looked up, surprised to see the Air Force colonel standing alongside of him. I would have expected him to be huddling inside his hummer.

"One KIA, one WIA. I think he can make it, but he needs immediate surgery for his arm. He'll lose that for sure, though."

"Can we leave him here for pick-up?" he asked me. "We've got to get the colonel here off the street and into the government center."

Before I could answer back, the colonel interrupted and said to me, "Don't worry about us there, son. If that man needs immediate assistance, then we're going to stay here until he gets it."

He turned to SSgt White and said, "Let's get this taken care of. I've got all you Marines here for security. Couldn't ask for more. So go ahead with the original plan. Get that wrecker in here to move the truck, and while that's being done, get that Iraqi back for treatment. We'll get there when we get there. I'm sure the governor will understand."

The platoon sergeant looked like he was going to argue, but then he nodded.

"You heard the colonel! Dunlop, Haddad! Get this man over to Doc's hummer, then get everyone back in their vehicles. Be ready for anything, and I mean anything!"

Pacman and Rob helped me move the Iraqi back to the hummer, where we laid him alongside of it in the shade. I looked up to see our male passenger leaning over the lap of the woman to peer down at us. I just ignored him.

It was almost 20 minutes before the wrecker came, accompanied by the battalion reaction force. My patient, my sniper, was taken off my hands while the wrecker physically yanked the front of the Iraqi truck around, slewing it sideways and opening up the road again.

I took a deep breath, then winced at the pain. I reached up to my chest, and my fingers felt a small lump in my flak jacket. I picked at it until I wrestled free a flattened piece of lead. This was the round that had hit me. It didn't seem that big, but without my body armor, and without it properly closed up, I would not have survived.

Before Sgt Butler kept on me about wearing my battle gear correctly, I would have loosened it. Would this round still have hit my armor, or would it have found the base of my neck? It was hard to tell, but it would have been close.

I had a feeling though, that even in death, Sgt Butler had saved my ass one more time.

Chapter 14

Hurricane Point
June 1, 2006

"You OK, Doc Cannon?" Umar asked as I held out my tray. "Mr. Rick, he tell me you got shot."

"Yea, I'm fine, Umar. Nothing happened."

Something had happened, though, and me being shot was a wake-up call. My mind hadn't been in the game, and that could have some pretty drastic consequences. The de facto camp motto of "complacency kills" was right on, even if my "complacency" might have been more of frustration mixed with anger. Either way, I hadn't been focusing on my job, and that was the key point.

There was no use getting Umar concerned, though. Umar was a fixture in the DFAC, a young Iraqi who bubbled over with enthusiasm for all things American, and the Marines in particular. He was especially taken with Rick. He had passable English, but with Rick, he kept trying to speak to him in Arabic, never grasping the fact that just because Rick was of Lebanese descent, he didn't speak the language. It seemed like his personal mission to bring Rick back into the fold, which was ironic as the kid was so anti-Iraq and pro-USA. When not on duty, he hung out around the camp, wearing the Tampa Bay Buccaneers t-shirt someone had given him. A few of the guys hated him, sure he was giving information to Al Qaeda. They were very obvious in their disdain, but for the most part, Umar was sort of our unofficial mascot.

I took my chili with rice, got a hunk of cornbread, filled my cup with bug juice, then went back to the table we normally claimed as our own. Conversation was already heavy on baseball, with Cy proclaiming loudly that the Twins were going to make a comeback.

"Yea, right," Pacman said. "What are they, 10, 11 games back of Detroit? In your dreams they come back."

I wasn't a huge fan. I'd go to a Padres game about once a year, but that was mostly just to have a night out. Last time I'd looked, the Pads were neck and neck with the Dodgers and Rockies in the division.

I sat down next to Cpl Dunlop and mostly tuned out the bickering.

"You OK, Doc?" he asked as I sat.

"Yea, no problem. Just a bruise. LT Henry cleared me."

"Well, you're pretty lucky. Another couple of inches, and bam!" he said, raising his voice for that last word.

"We weren't even a target, you know? The lieutenant told Mays that the truck driver wasn't involved. He's just a shitty driver who got stuck. The guys who shot you, they were just there to watch Michigan, and I guess one guy just got too excited and decided to try and take you out, the stupid fuck. He's already outta here to Balad, then it's Abu Ghraib for him, I bet." He paused for a second. "It sucks to be him.

"Good chili, by the way," he said as I took a bite.

I'm not sure what they called chili in Indiana, but I wasn't from Texas, and even I knew this chili was pretty weak. It was fuel for the body, but no way was it good. I nodded, though, then settled back to watch the others while I ate.

When I was a kid, after my older brother took off for God know where, meals were usually something thrown together that my mom and I ate in front of the TV. Eating with the same group of guys each day must be what it would be like to be part of a big family. Rick and Cpl Mays weren't there, but the rest of the squad was. The baseball argument was getting more heated, and the insults were flying, but none of that was serious. I think all of us really liked each other.

One of La'Ron's friends from Lima Company came up to him, slapping him on the back and initiating a convoluted but well choreographed fist bump. Mitchell, I think his name was, ignored the rest of us as he got on La'Ron's case about not hanging with his homeys. La'Ron promised to catch up with them later, and after another flurry of fist bumps, Mitchell left to eat his own lunch.

At Hurricane Point, there was some degree of racial grouping during free time. The brothers tended to hang out sometimes, along with some white brother wannabees, the Latinos hung out, the white guys hung out. The handful of Asians, though, seemed to gravitate between the brothers and the white guys. Part of the hanging out together was probably because of like interests, especially in music.

For the most part, though, we hung out in our units, especially in our squads. Sure, we bunked together, we worked together, but even beyond that, like here at chow, our squad, at least, stayed together. We may have had three black guys, an Asian, an Arab, a Latino, and six white guys, but, as hokey as it might sound, I felt we were all brothers from a different mother.

And if I couldn't get my head back in the game, I was a handicap, one who could end up costing one of the Marines in my care.

"Doc Cannon, the platoon sergeant wants to see you in the lieutenant's office," PFC Cherrystone interrupted my thoughts.

Second Squad was pretty close, but with Cherrydick standing there, I was struck with the thought that I was glad as hell that he wasn't in my squad. It was another reality check. Before my thoughts dove down too deep into mushiness and kumbaya, here was Cherrydick reminding me that not all of us were saints. Some were malingering dipwads.

Cherrydick claimed to have hurt his wrist, and Buster told me that it could have been a VERY slight sprain, but Cherrydick was milking it for all he was worth. This was his second "injury," and somehow, it just never seemed to heal. So he stayed back in the company office, acting as a runner.

"Sure thing, Cherrydick," I told him.

He got red in the face and said, "That's CherrySTONE, Doc."

"Oh yea, sure thing. Sorry about that. I'm coming," I told him, shoveling in one more mouthful of chili and rice.

I stood up as the rest of the guys laughed. I heard "fobbit" mentioned a few times, something Cherrydick heard, too, but he didn't have any outward reaction. "Fobbit" was a pretty severe insult to an infantry Marine, or any Marine, for that matter, but it was not surprising that he didn't have the gonads to take issue with the comments.

I didn't wait for him as I made my way to the company office. Lieutenant Hobbs had his own little office there that he shared with the other platoon commanders. The hatch was open, so I knocked on the door frame and stepped inside. Lieutenant Hobbs, SSgt White, and 1stLt Marez were inside. Both lieutenants excused themselves with my platoon commander closing the hatch after him, leaving me alone with SSgt White.

"Take a seat, there, Cannon," he told me, pointing to one of the mount-out boxes that served as a bench.

I wondered what this was all about.

SSgt White stared at me from over the small desk for a moment before beginning, "Doc, Cpl Mays tells me you've had a rough time of it lately. What's up?"

"Nothing, Staff Sergeant."

"Bullshit! I've watched you, too, and you've got a fucking chip on your shoulder the size of Alaska. And that, my friend, can get you killed."

I started to say something when he held up his hand, stopping me.

"I want you to take a look at this."

He turned his laptop around so I could see it and pressed the play on the Window Player that was up front. I scooted a little closer and saw a grainy video of a line of hummers out on some Iraqi street.

"Just watch," he told me as I started to ask him what this was.

The camera was not steady, and I could hear low voices speaking in Arabic. Just then, on one of the hummers, the one barely in the frame, the passenger door opened and someone stepped out. The camera suddenly centered on him, and the voices got a little more excited.

With a sudden realization, it hit me that the figure in the video was me. That was me getting out of the protection the hummer offered. That was me with a disgusted look on my face as I looked forward.

I looked up at the platoon sergeant, but he motioned me back to the screen. The voices got more excited, then they stopped talking. Only the heavy breathing of the cameraman could be heard.

The quiet lasted for about 15 seconds, then a shot rang out. On the screen, I fell to my knees, back up against the hummer. There was a shout of obvious exultation, then all chaos broke loose as La'Ron swung his .50 around and opened fire. Rounds peppered the scene for only a few seconds before the video stopped.

SSgt White slowly closed the laptop screen and swung it back to him. He sat there looking at me, waiting for me to say something. The problem was that I had nothing to say.

It must have been at least a full minute before he sighed and asked, "Just what the fuck do you think you were doing, Doc?"

"I, . . . I mean, . . . I don't know. I fucked up."

"'Fucked up' is putting it mildly! That was a fucking royal ass fuck up! Do you know, you weren't even a target? Those fuckheads weren't there for us—they were just observing, until you handed them their target of opportunity on a fucking silver platter!"

His voice as rising as he got more excited. And there was nothing I could say.

"What would have happened if Jarod or your buddy Haddad had gotten hit while trying to cover for you? Who would've taken care of them with you taking yourself out of the game like that? You not only put your own fucking worthless life on the line, but the lives of your entire squad, not to mention all the VIPs."

"I did treat that Iraqi," I mumbled quietly, not knowing what else to say.

"Only by shear fucking dumb luck. A better sniper and you'd be in a body bag right now heading for Dover."

He seemed to get a hold of himself and calmed down.

"Look, Sgt Butler was a hell of a Marine, a hell of a leader. I know you looked up to him."

He pulled out some papers, looking down at the top one.

"He kept notes on all of you. I copied these before we shipped his personal effects. Do you want to hear what he wrote about you?"

My heart skipped a beat. I wanted to shout out yes, but I wondered if I really wanted to know. Then I realized that for good or bad, I needed to know. I simply nodded, unable to get a word out.

"Let's see. OK, here is goes. 'HA Zachary Cannon, blah-blah-blah, boot size, gas mask size and so on.' Let me get to the better part. 'Immature, doesn't think things out. Accepts what others tell him. Only pays attention to his immediate tasks.'"

I swallowed. Was that what he thought of me? I know all of that was true, but I would have hoped that he held me in a little higher esteem.

"There's more: 'Loyal, capable, cares deeply for others. Courageous in the face of danger, tenacious in performing his job. Zach's a young corpsman, but he is ideally suited for the FMF. Talk to Doc Sylvester about him. Bring him on board.' He finishes with this: 'I REALLY like this young man.' He capitalized and underlined the 'REALLY'."

He put down the paper and looked at me expectantly.

I felt, well, I don't know what I felt. Relief? What?

"So Sgt Butler thought you are some sort of fucking super doc. What of it? If you've got your head up your ass so far because Sgt Butler got killed, then you are a fucking liability, and I'll send you back to the aid station so fast your eyes will burn. The platoon's lucky 'cause we've got three corpsmen. T/O's only for one, but here in Iraq, they know we're going to be in the shit, so they try and give us more. But I'll just keep Sylvester and Seychik if it comes to that. Better just two corpsmen I can trust than one whose going to get Marines killed.

"So what of it? Was Sgt Butler right? Or did you just blow smoke up his ass?"

"He was right," I murmured quietly.

"What was that? Say it like a man!"

"He was right!" I shouted out.

"Right about what, Doc?"

"Right about everything. I am immature, and I know it. I've been pissing and moaning ever since Sgt Butler was killed. I've been angry, and I've let it show. I almost got killed because of it, and I could have gotten others killed, too. But he was also right when he said I cared for the others. I care for my Marines, and if you try to take them from me, Staff Sergeant, I'm not going to let you. I'll request mast to the commanding general if I have to. Sgt Butler wrote I was tenacious, and believe you me, if you want to see how tenacious, just try and fire me."

I had stood up while going off, and I leaned over his desk, breathing hard. I had to struggle to hold back my emotions. I suddenly realized what I was doing, that I was yelling, that I was threatening a SNCO. I stepped back away from him, waiting for his inevitable explosion.

"OK, then, that's what I wanted to hear. I'll keep you with your squad, but Cpl Mays and I'll be watching you," he said calmly.

"Sgt Butler was a hell of a Marine, and we all mourn his loss. I understand what you're going through." He leaned back, eyes closed. "You know, this is one fucked up job. It's hard to take. I love the Corps with all my heart. It's my life, you know. The Marines, and that includes our corpsmen, they are the best men in the fucking universe. But when people like Derek get killed, like so many others I've known have been killed, I have to wonder about it all. What a fucking waste," he continued sadly, more to himself than to me.

He seemed to get a hold of himself, and the brash, foul-mouthed platoon sergeant was back.

"Get your ass back to your hootch. You've got another fucking patrol tonight, and you better not fuck it up.

I turned and opened the hatch. Halfway through it, I turned back and said "Thank you" before going to join the rest of my squad.

Chapter 15

Ramadi
June 5, 2006

I was out with Third Squad and not particularly happy about it. Kilo had deployed with 11 corpsmen, but with Sean Gruber KIA and now HM2 Sylvester down hard with a respiratory infection, the company was down to nine effective corpsmen, and it was up to Buster and me to cover the platoon. Sylvester was the platoon corpsman, but he was also dual-hatted Third Squad's. We had 21 corpsmen in the Aid Station Group, and while sometimes they would help out in the field, this time no one was supposedly available.

I had nothing against Third Squad, but that left Second Squad, my squad, uncovered. They were standing gate watch for the day, so they could get help from the aid station if someone got hit, but still, they were *my* Marines, and I wanted to be with them.

Sgt Castanza hadn't blinked an eye, though, when he was told he would have me, a mere HA, with him instead of the more experienced Sylvester. I appreciated that, at least.

We really didn't expect much to happen on this trip, anyway. We had escorted some Army major and a civilian to the government center, dropped them off, and were headed back to Hurricane Point. The stress level was much lower in the daylight. Attacks were not as common as at night, and we could see the signs of IEDs much easier. And in this case, we'd just come down Michigan only 30 minutes before, so we knew the way was clear, at least of IEDs.

As we made our way north, I looked out the window of the hummer. The place looked deserted. I wondered where all the people were, where they spent their time. This was a pretty big city, but we rarely saw many people when we were out there. I knew they saw us, though. There were probably multiple sets of eyes on us at that very moment.

Between Hurricane Point and the government center, on the west side of Michigan, was half of a small building. It looked like Godzilla had taken the missing half of the building out in one bite. I always wondered what had made that shape—a huge, fairly even crescent—it was just too geometrical. I thought Godzilla was just as logical as anything else. To me, though, the Godzilla building was my landmark that we were halfway back.

I turned to look at the building as we drove past when an explosion sounded in front of us. I spun around, thinking our lead vehicle had been hit. But the explosion was further forward, and the radio chatter confirmed that it was up ahead. Firing rang out, the deeper chatter of an M242 25mm chain gun mixing in with the M240 7.62 machine guns and small arms. The Marines were light on LAVs, so that meant it was probably an Army unit getting hit just ahead of us. Sgt Castanza would know who was on the route, but me sitting in the back of the fourth hummer in the convoy, well, no one was rushing to keep me informed as to what was happening.

We initially stopped when we heard the explosion. The insurgents often would plant secondary IEDs to get us when we rushed to help someone else. But after only a few moments, Sgt Castanza ordered us forward. After another few moments, the wounded Bradley was in front of us, a small amount of smoke drifting up. Two more Bradleys were in position, guns tracking, but no longer firing. We pulled into as much of an arc as the width of the street would allow.

The radio chatter was incessant, but I tuned it out as I peered forward to the Bradley, wondering if anyone was hurt. While not a tank, it was still a pretty robust vehicle, and from what I'd heard, they often just brushed off IED attacks.

The Bradley had a turret right on top, and the hatch on top of that opened. A head stuck out, arm waving. I was focusing on him, wondering what was happening.

"Doc! Didn't you hear that? They need you out there!" shouted Cpl Redding from the front seat.

I didn't hesitate. I pushed open the door and ran over to the front of the Bradley, joined by Sgt Castanza, Cpl Harris, and Kyle Van Meter. I was looking up at the guy in the turret, and I could see he was going into shock. I started to climb up when a couple of soldiers ran around from in back of the Bradley.

"Over here," one of the shouted, waving his arm wildly to get our attention.

We rushed around to join them.

"You've got your medic? Ours is in there" one of the soldiers asked wildly.

I raised my hand as Sgt Castanza pushed me forward.

Almost absently, I noticed that he was a lieutenant. Just as absently, I took in the couple of soldiers providing security, arms pointing outwards. That calmed me some. Even if the lieutenant was excited, those soldiers looked pretty professional. The Bradley looked intact, so any injuries should be minor.

I was wrong.

I came around the back of the Bradley and stepped up and through the round open hatch. Inside, the smell hit me first, the coppery smell of blood, the foul smell of shit and body parts. Then, well, as my eyes adjusted to the dim light, it took my mind precious moments to register what I was seeing. As a kid, I used to read detective books, and quite often, horrific crime scenes were described as looking like an "abattoir." I always wondered at that description, but it all suddenly came into focus. That is what the inside of the Bradley looked like.

There was a fairly large hole up high on the side of the vehicle. Whatever made it had wrecked havoc inside the compartment and to the soldiers who had been inside. Body parts and blood covered almost every square inch of it. I took a step and almost slipped on bloody tissue, tissue I couldn't even place. I started to blanch in the face of the horror, actually taking a step back.

"Gail, . . ." a voice weakly called out just to my right.

That focused me. I needed to snap to. This was my job.

"Get an air casevac in here now!" I shouted out to those behind me.

Triage was my first priority. I had to find out who had the best chance of being saved. I knelt next to the man who had called out for Gail. Half of his face was gone, his arm was gone, and his chest was a tangled mass of damaged flesh. He wouldn't make it. I left him to check on the next body. I flipped him over. His head was gone. The next man was dead, too, his back and chest a mangled mass of hamburger. I saw the patch that the Army medics wore on his tattered uniform, but I let that slide past me. The next solder was alive, but unconscious. I did a very quick assessment. He was bleeding, but not seriously. His neck was stable, so I pulled him towards the back where Cpl Harris, the Army lieutenant, and another soldier were looking in the open hatch.

"You," I ordered the lieutenant, "get him out of here. He's got a concussion, maybe more. Lay him down and then don't move him."

I turned back inside. The next body wasn't a body, just two legs connected at the hips. There was nothing whole above that. I tried not to look too closely, steeling my emotions.

From above me, light was coming in the open turret hatch. Blocking the way, though, was a groaning soldier. I could see that both of his feet were gone, the top of his right boot still tied around his lower leg. Whatever had taken out his feet had cut the lower part of his boot right off. I helped him ease back down into the compartment. He was conscious, but very much in shock. I did a quick assessment. Other than his feet, he didn't look hurt.

"Cpl Harris, get in here!" I shouted.

I should have checked the remaining soldiers, but I didn't want this guy to bleed out. I applied two quick tourniquets around his stumps, then told Harris to grab someone and pull the wounded soldier out of the Bradley. I knew these vehicles had fire suppression systems, but I kept getting flashes in my mind of the thing going up into flames.

To the left of the soldier I'd just pulled out was another soldier. He was conscious, but barely so. He was moving, so I left him there to check on anyone else. In the front of the compartment, was one more soldier. He was alive, but his right shoulder was hanging on by a thread. Descending from it was a mangled mass of flesh. Looking back at the hole in the Bradley, I figured he had been sitting facing where they had been hit, but far enough forward that he didn't bear the full brunt of whatever hit them.

Even with his arm mangled, he wasn't bleeding too badly. He had other injuries, but he was pretty lucky. I picked him up, carefully stepping though the blood and grime, not wanting to think of all of that, but not wanting to slip and drop the soldier, either. I handed him off to eager waiting hands waiting for me.

"I need two men here, now," I shouted out.

Kyle and a soldier jumped in, neither looking to the sides at the carnage but focusing solely on me.

"There's a guy up past that turret. He looks like he isn't too badly hurt, but bring him out carefully. I'll check him when he's out."

I looked around. That was seven soldiers.

"Hey," I called out to the soldier, "how many of you in one of these?"

"Nine. Three crew and six pax."

I looked around. There were body parts and pieces all around me. Did they make up the missing two men?

I turned back to the man who had first called out for "Gail." I wondered who she was. A wife? A lover? A daughter?

I knelt beside him. He was still alive, and even partially conscious. I didn't know how much longer he would be. There was nothing I could do but to ease his pain. I took out my kit and gave him a shot of morphine, leaving him in place. Moving him could kill him.

I stepped out to check on the others. Another soldier had joined the rest, but he hadn't any weapons and was covered in dirt and soot. He looked up as I came out.

"The rest . . .?" he pleaded.

I shook my head.

Sgt Castanza came up to me. "He's the driver. Came out his hatch. Doesn't look hurt, but you might want to check him over. We've got two birds incoming, ETA about two minutes."

With only two minutes, I wanted to make sure my patients were ready for transport. Number one would be the soldier who had lost his feet. But if they were Black Hawks, I knew we could get all the WIAs in one load.

"Can we lower the whole ramp on that Bradley" I asked the lieutenant.

"Sure thing," he answered, then telling one of the soldiers to get it done. The first soldier jumped up and reached inside the open hatch, only to reel away and kneel to throw up in the road. An older soldier stepped up and reached inside. The hatch began to lower, bringing in more light to the scene inside. There were more than a few gasps from the assembled men as they saw what had happened to their buddies.

The first of the Black Hawks settled down beside one of the remaining Bradleys. The crew chief jumped out and was briefed by a soldier who ran up to him. He nodded and started to pull out the mobile stretchers they had onboard.

About ten soldiers and three Marines helped load the wounded onto the bird. Anderson, the one who had called out for Gail, was the last to go. I had read his name on his flak jacket when the ramp went down. I wondered if that was a good thing or not. He was clinging to life, but he couldn't last much longer, and now that I knew his name, his passing would have more impact on me.

As they lifted off, my adrenalin rush left me. I looked back up at the Bradley. Something had punched right through the side armor, up high. I'd heard the insurgents had a new kind of IED, where they used a steel plate as a projectile, and this looked like it might be that type. It being high would explain the injuries to the heads and upper bodies of the soldiers who had been seated inside.

I wondered how the insurgents had managed to get whatever it was between the time we first passed on the way to the government house and the time we came back. Then it hit me. It had been there all along. It was just that in a hummer, we weren't an important enough target. This was a test, to see if they could take out something bigger. They had watched us drive by and passed us up.

The thought hit me hard. I looked down at myself, completely covered in gore. But for the grace of God, that could have been us. The Ready First soldiers had been unlucky enough to be guinea pigs for new Al Qaeda tactics.

Other elements of the Army arrived, including one of their Voodoo Mobiles, the ambulances they made out of the old M113s. It was a pretty smart use of old gear, I thought, creating a way to get casualties out of a hot zone, even if this time, we'd used air assets. With the Army having things well in hand, Sgt Castanza rounded us up for the trip back. Before I could get back into my hummer, though, the lieutenant and a sergeant first class came up to me. They shook my hand, and the SFC handed me a coin. The Army loved to hand out coins, and this one probably had their unit on it, but I was too frazzled to really look at it.

"Thanks, doc. We appreciate what you did. You ever get over to Camp Ramadi, you look us up, OK?" the SFC said. "We mean it."

"It was nothing," I said automatically before realizing that might come out right. "I'm sorry, I didn't mean that all of this was nothing."

"We know what you mean," he reassured me. "But you were something. We always take care of our own, and with Blanchard KIA, we're lucky you and your Marines were nearby so you could take his place and help us. From the bottom of our hearts, we thank you."

I watched them as they turned around and went back to the remainder of their unit.

A hand was put on my shoulder. "Come on, doc, let's get home.

I would never have thought of Camp Hurricane as home, but for now, I could accept that. I opened the door of the hummer and got inside, ready to get back, take a shower, and maybe get a call into Amy.

Chapter 16

Ramadi
June 11, 2006

There was a new sheriff in town. We'd been briefed that the Ready First's commander wanted to take it to the Iraqis, but I think most of us thought that after a couple of weeks, some of that would fade away. If anything, the tempo was increasing. We were going on more patrols and more kinds of patrols. They even had India out there running some patrols in boats, cruising up and down the river. More action, though, meant more casualties. There were more Hero Flights, more memorial services.

So far, the platoon had been lucky. We'd had no serious casualties for a couple of weeks, just one sprained ankle and a back injury. Considering the weight we carried and how we were jumping walls, going in windows, and all of that, I was surprised we weren't getting more muscular-skeletal injuries. The wear and tear was pretty serious, though. I figured the VA would be having its hands full with claims as the years went on. These issues would be the Iraq War's Agent Orange.

"We've got a blood trail," La'Ron said as he came back to report to Cpl Mays. "It looks like he's bleeding pretty good."

"OK, let's follow it and see where it leads," the squad leader told him.

We were close to the edge of our battle area. We'd gotten word that an Army sniper had hit an insurgent, but the man had stumbled back and into our AOR. Normally, we coordinated hot pursuit between units, but since the platoon was in the area, the Army informed us and left it to us to find the guy. It made sense to me. We knew the area better, and anything that lessened the chances for friendly fire was a good thing.

The platoon was spread out, moving slowly, each squad in a stack doing a block-by-block search. It hadn't taken long; after only twenty minutes or so, our point had hit the blood trail.

The tension in the squad immediately went up a notch. We wanted to be the ones who captured the guy.

I moved slightly ahead so I was just in back of Rick's team. We knew the guy was hurt, but not how badly. If he was really messed up, it was up to me to keep him alive until we could get him back to the ITT team.

Up ahead, I saw Jerry Scanlon hold up his fist. We all froze. He motioned for Rick to move forward, and the two of them conferred. I wished I knew what they were saying.

Rick looked back, then made some hand and arm signals. The blood trail led into one of the buildings. Cpl Mays carefully moved forward, and when he reached me, I followed in his wake. We made it up to Third Team and crouched down behind the wall in front of the building.

"We've got blood going in the front door. There's no sign of anything else," Rick told the squad leader.

Cpl Mays did a quick bob up and down, seeing for himself what Rick had told him. He told Rick we would be clearing the house. He motioned for the two other fire team leaders, then called the lieutenant to let him know what was happening. Lieutenant Hobbs told him to go ahead, but to wait until the other two squads could get into position to support us with security and overwatch. With the houses in Ramadi so close together, it was easy for insurgents to move from one house to another while Marines were clearing the first one, so someone had to keep an eye on what was going on.

"OK, we've done this a million times. Nothing new here. We've maybe got a wounded or dead insurgent inside. We don't know who else might be there. Heads up, and think, think, think. First, you're still the assault team. You're in first, and you clear to the left. Second, you're still support. I want you in on First's heels. Split the stack and clear to the right. Third, make sure the bottom floor is cleared, then keep it secure. We don't need anyone coming up our butts from outside. After that, use our footholds and just talk it out. If we take a casualty, be ready to flood the house or break contact on my order. There's no room for mistakes here. Remember, 'tactical patience!'"

The "book" pushed for a top down assault, that is, going in on the roof and working our way down a building. This tended to limit the egress routes the guerillas used to make their getaway were easier to cover by the support element, and we could use grenades by throwing them down instead of up. For the martyr types, the insurgents who didn't expect to live but who wanted to take out as many of us as possible, they tended to barricade themselves in rooms and stairwells, and coming down at them was easier than fighting up.

For me, though, as a corpsmen, I hated top-down assaults. If someone was hit, getting them out of the fight by hauling them back up ladderwells was pretty tough. It hadn't happened to me yet, but I'd heard all about it.

Top down or bottom up, guerilla or martyr, clearing a building was one of the more harrowing things we had to do in Iraq. The idea that right behind a door was a machine gun ready to take you out was always on your mind. Out in the street, there was a sense of distance, and even if they shot at you, there was room to move. But in some small bedroom, not even an Iraqi could miss. The first guy into a room was at serious risk of getting taken out.

We all moved into position, and when given the OK from the platoon commander, we rushed through the gate and up to the front door. Jerry ran his hands along it, looking for any sign of a booby trap. He reached the knob and twisted, but it didn't move. It was locked. There went the first part of our subdued entry. I wondered if Cpl Mays would change it to a dynamic entry, with us yelling and firing, tossing grenades as we went. But then again, if we were trying to capture someone, that probably wasn't the best way to go about it, unless we just wanted a body.

The Marines Corps had a hundred ways to breach a door, some of them pretty high tech. But for a rifle squad, it usually boiled down to the Mark 1 Mod 1 boot, a hooligan, or shooting out the lock with a shotgun or M16. An M203 was effective, but friendlies had to be pretty far back before one was used. SMAWs worked great, too, but a squad didn't always have access to one, and the same problem about standoff distance was there. We also carried an "eight ball," which was a 1/8 stick of C4, but the same problems of us getting out of the way made this less than the preferred course of action.

In this case, Jerry decided to use the Mossberg. He shouldered his M16, unlimbered the shotgun, and holding the muzzle down at an angle and touching the locking mechanism, sent one of the big Lockbuster-C slugs into the door. The door didn't have a chance and flopped open.

Immediately, First Fire Team rushed in, just as they'd practiced hundreds of times back at Lejeune and the Stumps. Even after all this time with the unit, it still gave me a bit of a thrill to watch them work like that, as if they were all connected somehow. Second Team rushed in right behind them. I was on their heels. Like most houses, the front door led to a small entry with two small sitting rooms alongside it. Two interior doors led to other rooms with a main hallway running to the back of the building. These interior doors could almost always be just kicked in, and Pacman had already breached one of them. There was a stairway going up to the right, and a quick glance showed me blood going up them. Cpl Dunlop saw the blood too, but he needed to clear the bottom floor. Just because we saw the blood didn't mean that someone else wasn't downstairs ready to hit us, or even if the wounded insurgent hadn't doubled back.

"Coming in!" Steve Jenner shouted as First Fire Team entered the building. They were the security element. Cpl Choi put his two Marines on the ladderwell, weapons pointing up it.

"Clear!" shouted Jerry to the left.

As usual, the point man called out what he was seeing. All of us were supposed to shut up and listen.

"Hold left, clear right!" shouted out Cpl Mays, letting First know to hold up until Second cleared their sector.

In MOUT operations, no one was ever left alone. It was always the buddy system. With Cpl Mays as the squad leader, neither of us had an actual combat buddy, so we were wedded together for the course of the action.

The shouts of "Next man in left," "Coming out," "Clear," "Move," and such were an ongoing newsflash of how things were progressing. In just a few minutes, the shout of "All clear!" let us know that the bottom floor was secure. We turned to look at the ladderwell.

Going up stairwells was one of the most dicey parts of clearing a building. The way was restricted, and anything could come tumbling down on you. Cpl Mays gave Rick the signal to move out. The four Marines in the team started the choreographed movement up the stairs, each move designed to keep the entire area covered. There could be no area that would put us in danger. Despite the dirty, sweaty Marines being loaded down with gear, it was almost a ballet.

I just hugged the outside wall, following Cpl Mays up, my M16 at the ready. We made it to the top of the stairs without incident and faced a long hallway. Once again, Cpl Mays split the stack, sending First to the rooms on the right, Second to the rooms on the left. Cy Pierce peeled off and stayed with us, his SAW providing security down the length of the hallway.

We found our insurgent in the first room to the right.

Pacman and LCpl Jarod moved in, then immediately called out, "Here he is!"

Cpl Mays and I rushed in. It was small room, maybe 8 feet by 6 feet. Up against the side wall near the back was a small wardrobe that had seen better days. On the floor, up against the far wall under the window, was a middle aged man, his arm a bloody mess. His white cotton shirt was stained crimson. He looked like he had been trying to reach the window, but his body had just given out. He was panting and looking up to us, an almost feral expression of a trapped animal in his face. I shouldered my M16 and started to move forward, but Cpl Mays held his arm our across my chest, stopping me.

I was surprised for a second, but as Pacman started to search the man, I felt embarrassed. It wasn't just a few people in the fight who had been taken out by wounded men who suicided when someone came close.

Pacman gave the all clear, so I moved forward. I picked up the man's wrist to take a look. He never even flinched, but I could see he was in serious pain. The Army sniper's round had hit the man right in the back of the elbow, making a hash out of the joint. Even a cursory glance made it clear that this elbow would never work again, and that the arm would probably come off. His elbow stood in stark contrast to the hand below the hamburger of a joint. Aside from a stream of blood that had run down it, the hand was clean. There wasn't even any dirt under his fingernails. I had figured that if he was shot, he must have been emplacing an IED or something, but this man hadn't been digging anything.

I did a full assessment. He was in obvious pain, and his pulse was racing, but the only injury was to his arm.

"He's going to make it," I told Cpl Mays.

"OK, well, patch him up, and we'll get him out of here. You two," he told Jarod and Pacman, stay here with the doc. We still need to clear the rest of the building."

With that he stepped out, joining the rest of the squad.

It was hard to treat the man up against the wall, so I pulled him out to the middle of the small room. He didn't resist, but I could see him tense up as his arm touched the floor. I knew he was in some serious pain, so first, I decided to give him a shot of morphine. I reached in my kit and pulled out the pre-loaded syringe, tapping it to get rid of the air bubbles.

"Pacman, get back from the window," Jarod said.

I looked up where Pacman had sidled to the edge of the window to look out. He made a sheepish grin, then stepped back, bumping into the small wardrobe that was up against the wall.

As soon as he did that, the door to the wardrobe flew open, and a shape burst out, knocking him flat. I was barely aware of what was happening, but I reacted by instinct. With Pacman down on the floor and me between Jarod and the guy who had exploded from the wardrobe, I spun around, syringe in my hand, backhanding him as hard as I could and burying the syringe into the stomach of the Iraqi as he tried to rush past me.

The guy folded and collapsed on the floor, probably more from the shock of my fist in his gut than from the syringe. Jarod stepped up, weapon trained on the man as I slowly stood up.

"Holy shit, Doc! You took him out with your fucking hypo!" he exclaimed slowly.

"Coming in!" shouted Cpl Mays as he and Cy rushed back into the room. He took in the gasping Iraqi on the floor, then the open wardrobe door.

"You didn't clear that thing?" he shouted. "What's your fifth step of room clearing?"

He was almost frothing at the mouth, he was so upset.

"Search the room," the two answered in unison.

"That's right! Search the fucking room!"

I don't think I'd ever heard Cpl Mays curse before. I hoped I wouldn't become one of his targets. I was in the room, too, after all.

"I . . . I . . . just search him, at least! Get this room secure! Coming out!" he managed to get out before wheeling out of the room.

Pacman and Jarod looked at each other, shrugged their shoulders, and let out a big breath of air. Pacman got up and searched the new man who seemed to realize that he wasn't really hurt that much. Oh, he had a four-inch syringe embedded in his stomach, but mostly, he'd just had the breath knocked out of him. I pulled out the syringe, then unlimbered my M16 and held it on the man until Pacman had him zip-cuffed. Then it was back to the original Iraqi, the one who'd been shot in the first place.

I took out another syringe, the first one being ruined.

"Man oh man," Jarod said with what sounded an impressed tone of voice, "Combat Doc here's nailed his first raghead, and with a hypo, no less. That's some serious shit!"

"Amen to that" Pacman joined in.

I didn't know what to say, so I just did what I knew how to do. I treated my patient.

Chapter 17

Hurricane Point
June 20, 2006

"Hey Zach, Senior Chief wants to see you."

I looked up to Cpl Morrison, the company clerk.

What the heck does he want? I wondered.

"He said make it snappy."

"OK, OK. I'm on my way."

I really wanted to do anything other than going to see how I'd screwed up. We'd been out all night, and I spent the morning at sick call and cleaning my weapon. I just wanted to catch a few Z's before lunch. Today was my birthday, not that it meant anything here. But I'd call Amy later, when it was the 20th back home, time difference and all that.

I wearily put my gear back on wondering if I had time to hit the head first, but deciding that no, I needed to get whatever it was over with. I went into the aid station and asked HM3 Krytpos where senior chief was.

"He's in a meeting. You can park it over there if you need to see him," he told me.

"He wants to see me, not the other way around."

"Don't know anything about that," he said as he went back to his paperwork.

So I sat down and waited. And waited. Twenty minutes went by, and no senior chief. I started drifting off; it'd had been a long night, after all. When someone collapsed in the chair beside me, I jumped up, but it was only Rocket.

HM Pauling was a whining-type corpsman who made no bones that he hated it with the Marines. He was a big tall guy, but he was soft, like the Pillsbury Doughboy. He was in his full battle gear, dirty and beat. He'd obviously been augmenting one of the platoons on a patrol overnight.

"I don't know . . . how you put up . . . with this shit," he said to me, the words coming between big intakes of air.

"Ah, it's a job," I responded.

Truth be told, I was a little ashamed of Rocket. I thought he made all corpsmen look bad. I wanted to tell him to just suck it up.

Jonathan P. Brazee

"I'll be so glad when this tour is over. Then it's back to the fleet for me. You still want to be a radiology tech?" he asked.

"Yea, that's the plan," I said.

"Then no more of the Marine bullshit, right? That'll be sweet, right?"

"Yea, I guess."

I wanted to tell him it wasn't bullshit. I still planned on getting the training I needed to get a good job for my family. No more living with my mom. But being with the Marines wasn't "bullshit." I would remember my time with them. I didn't say that, though. I just sat there, not really understanding why I didn't stick up for my buddies.

Rocket chattered on for awhile, probably too beat to get up and get his gear squared away. Senior Chief finally came out and rescued me from him.

"You want to see me, Cannon?" he asked.

"No, Senior Chief, I was told you wanted to see me?"

"Now why would I want to see your sorry ass, there? You trying to get out of some company duty?"

I was confused.

"No, no. Cpl Morrison said you wanted to see me right away. You don't want to see me?"

"You think I don't know who I want to see and who I don't want to see? Let me give you a hint: I don't want to see you. Get back to your company and back to work."

With that, he spun around and went back into his office.

I didn't know what the heck was going on. Was Morrison messing with me, or maybe the word just got mixed up.

I shook my head and started out.

"See, even the career FMF corpsmen are just as fucked up as the Marines," Rocket said as I walked past him and out the hatch.

I walked back to the company SWA, ready to confront Morrison. Rick caught me though, limping.

"Hey Zach, can you check out my foot? It's hurting pretty bad."

I looked over to the company CP, wanting to grab Morrison, but my Marines had to come first, especially Rick.

"Sure," I said, following him back to our hootch. He opened the hatch, stepping aside and waiting for me to enter.

"Surprise! Happy Birthday!"

It looked like the entire platoon was crammed into our squadbay. A couple of the other corpsmen from the company were there, too.

La'Ron had a big knife in his hand, standing in back of the hootch's only table. On the table was a pitcher of bug juice and a cake.

"Come cut your cake. It's looking mighty delish sitting there."

I almost felt overcome. I looked out at the faces, and all I could see was a true welcome. I had the sudden urge to run back to the aid station and grab Rocket, tell him that this wasn't all bullshit. But to him, maybe it was. He didn't have Marines, brothers like this, who would get a cake out in the middle of the Sandbox for him.

"Where'd you get the cake?" I asked as I walked up, hands pounding my shoulders.

"Umar got it for you. He got all the chow for us," Rick said, his limp miraculously gone.

Umar was standing there beside La'Ron, beaming. I knew he did it as a favor for Rick, but I still appreciated it.

As I got to the cake, I had to stop. It was a flat pan cake, with bits of chocolate peeking out beneath the white frosting. Umar had decorated it, though. Beside the "Happy Birthday Doc Cannon," there was an image of someone obviously meant to be me. In his hand was a huge syringe, and he was in the process of hitting a caricature of an Arab, complete with robes and a camel in the background.

I had to laugh as calls of "OoRah!" and "Combat Doc!" rang out.

I was still pretty embarrassed by the incident. The man I'd stuck wasn't really an insurgent. He was just the brother of the guy who'd been shot—but that man was insurgent, at least. But insurgent or not, the rest of the guys in the platoon, heck in the rest of the battalion, seemed to love it. I knew I had to take it with good grace.

At the repeated urgings of the others, most stridently from La'Ron, I cut the cake. The privates and the PFCs got theirs first, and then up the ranks. Senior Chief made it in in time to get his before the lieutenant. He was laughing, so I knew he'd been in on it all the time. I was surprised that Capt Wilcox, the first sergeant, and the gunny even stopped by for a few minutes.

After everyone else was served, I got my own piece of cake. I took a big bite. It was surprisingly good, Iraq or not.

"Happy birthday there, bud," Rick said as he took a seat beside me on my rack.

I looked around at everybody, some starting to leave the hootch, to get back to the war. I was away from my Amy, from my son. I was in the middle of the desert, where people would be happy to kill me. I was dirty, tired, and exhausted. But somehow, this birthday had to rank up there as one of my best.

"Damn fine birthday," I told him.

"Yea, not bad," he agreed. "You're still not old enough to order a beer, though, youngun!"

Chapter 18

Ramadi
July 1, 2006

The loudspeakers blared out their taunts in Arabic. I couldn't understand each phrase, but Azar had enthusiastically told us that they meant things like "Are you a man? Then come prove it to us. Come fight!" and "Only women hide like rats, afraid to fight."

"So, are they coming?" La'Ron called down from where he crouched in the gun turret.

He wasn't exposing himself to any sniper, but he was ready to pop up and fire if the attack came.

"If they've got balls, they will," Cpl Choi answered. "Thems some pretty heavy insults we're throwing their way."

We had taken on a new tactic. Instead of trying to dig the bad guy out, we were daring them to come meet us. We called it being "fly bait." One of the Ready First battalions had done this last week, and 14 Iraqis had died trying to prove their manhood.

This was a company operation. Our entire platoon was arranged in one of the squares, ready and waiting. The other platoons were deployed within a few blocks of us. We had a Bradley with us, and their chain gun was a nice piece of insurance. Back at Lejeune and at the stumps, we'd worked with the Marines' LAVs, but the LAV battalion was up at Ar Rutbah conducting their own operations out in the open desert. Among all of us hummers, the Bradley looked like a beast, even if it was dwarfed by the M1s that the BCT had. There was an M1 with First Platoon, one of the four Marine tanks in Ramadi, but Third and us had Army Bradleys.

As I glanced at it, though, I couldn't help but think about the last time I had been in one. It wasn't a pleasant thought.

"I wished they'd get it on. I've got to take a wicked piss," La'Ron remarked.

Cpl Choi just handed him up an empty water bottle. La'Ron took it and kept it for when he really couldn't wait any longer.

We'd been sitting there for about two hours. The sun was up and beating down on us; we were burning hot. I wanted to undo the neck of my flak jacket, but each time my gloved hand unconsciously reached up, I thought of Sgt Butler. That stopped my hand each time.

A loud rasping snore filled the cab of the hummer.

"Jenner! Wake the fuck up!" shouted Choi, smacking Steve on the shoulder.

Steve was the driver, and he'd actually fallen asleep. He shook the sleep out of his eyes.

"I wasn't asleep," he protested.

"Yea, that was just an Iraqi frog farting we heard there," La'Ron said, sticking his head down.

He reached back and I gave him the obligatory fist bump.

"Yea Doc, he knows."

I wasn't entirely sure what he meant by that, but I bumped fists with him again anyway.

"I wasn't asleep," Steve muttered to no one in particular.

A single shot rang out from somewhere above us. La'Ron jumped back up into his turret as we spun our heads looking around.

Across the street from us, a body lay inside a doorway. It was only 15 or 20 meters from us, so we could easily see the packed explosives around his torso.

A fucking suicide bomber!

The thought chilled me. IEDs were bad enough, but suicide bombers were like guided IEDs. We hadn't had that many of them yet, but Al Qaeda's use of them was increasing.

I spun my head to try and look up over us. One of the emplaced snipers had just taken the guy out. He hadn't even made it one step into the street, so the sniper must have been watching him, and when the bomber made his move, our sniper sent him to his 79 virgins, even if a tiny bit earlier than when he wanted to go to Paradise.

Sporadic fire broke out. The suicide bomber was probably supposed to signal the start of an attack, but when he was taken out, it took the insurgents a few moments to get going.

It didn't take the platoon a few moments to respond, though. Almost immediately, all the gunners on the turrets opened up, and the Bradley's chain gun and 240 machine gun their contribution. The noise was tremendous, sound waves bouncing back and forth from either side of the square. Within moments, dust and smoke obscured our vision. I had my weapon at the ready, but unless someone came running out of the smoke at us, this was going to be a battle of our mounted weapons.

I had been with the Marines for a little over half a year, but this was the most concentrated fire I'd ever experienced. We'd blown off rounds at the range back in the US, but this was different. We were firing these rounds with evil intent.

After almost a minute, the radio crackled with the command to cease fire. Cpl Choi slapped La'Ron's leg to get his attention.

My ears were ringing as silence took over. It took awhile for things to come into view, vehicle shapes emerging slowly as the dust settled. Around us, there was no movement. The buildings, never in good shape in this city, had absorbed a tremendous amount of damage, the firing chewing up the walls. Whole sections had been shot out. We hadn't even used indirect fire, and the Bradley hadn't fired their TOW, but you could have fooled me on that based on the degree of damage I saw.

It was up to First and Third to check our damage. We remained as the security element, covering the other two squads.

The two squads pulled out six broken bodies, laying them out on the dirt of the square. The suicide bomber was left in place for EOD. Blood seeped out from under the bodies, at first bright red, but then dulling as dust rose to cover the blood's surface. Even under the bright sunlight, everything took on a washed out hue.

Seven men couldn't take the insults and had rushed to prove their manhood. Now they were just mangled meat.

Chapter 19

Hurricane Point
July 4ᵗʰ, 2006

"The first sergeant told me to give this to you," Cpl Morrison said after walking into the hootch, handing me a piece of paper.

"What's this?" I asked.

"I guess you're gonna hafta read it," he said.

I looked it over. It was a cover sheet from the Department of the Army.

What would I care about the Army?

I read on. I saw the brigade commander's name there, then mine. I got to the subject.

"Well, shit," was all I could say.

"What do you got?" newly promoted Corporal Richard S. Haddad asked.

"The Army's giving me a friggin' medal," I told him.

"What?" came from him and several of the other guys.

We'd all just come back from chow, a July 4ᵗʰ feast of steak, chicken, burgers, corn-on-the-cob, even fresh watermelon. They got up off their racks and came to look over my shoulder.

"It says right here that I'm getting the Army Achievement Medal for that shit with the Bradley that was hit. Says my actions were 'exemplary.' Look here, it even says that I 'prevented further loss of life.'"

"Well no shit, Doc. Fuckin' A," Rick said, grabbing the paper from my hand.

"But I didn't save anyone's life. I just gave basic care, and that Spec 4, Anderson? I didn't think he was going to make it, and I never gave him any care until after all the rest."

"But he did make it, right? And he's back in Germany or the States, now, right?"

"Yea, but . . ."

"There're no 'buts' about it. You done good. And if the Army wants to give you a medal for that, all the better."

"You'll get the medal and certificate at the awards presentation. The sergeant major said the CO wants to pin it on you," Morrison said.

He looked around as the cover sheet made the rounds of the others. His voice went down a few decibels.

"Did you hear?"

Cpl Morrison was a conscientious, hard-working Marine, stuck in the company office as the clerk. Working for the first sergeant was something none of us would want, so we all had a better you than me attitude when he came around. One more thing, though, was that he was a big-time gossip. He heard things. When we heard his standard opening of "Did you hear?" we usually rolled our eyes—Marines didn't listen to gossip, right?-- but that never stopped us from listening in.

"Over at Fallujah, the Iraqis, they captured one of the Marines there, we think."

We didn't make any pretense of belittling what he told us. This was serious shit, something probably everyone one of us thought about and feared.

Our combined exclamations drowned each other out.

"Yep. Right outside their government center. One of the convoys got hit, and a corporal's gone missing."

"Maybe he's laying low?" Pacman asked, almost hopefully.

"The word is that they found drag marks, and they think he's been taken."

"Well, he'll be starring on the Al Qaeda You-Tube right ricky-tic," Jarod said sourly.

"Oh you mother," and "shut the fuck up," were shouted at him, along with a boot being hurled.

"What? You all know what's going to happen," he said in protest.

LCpl Bret Jarod was a good enough Marine, but the guy had no social skills. That was probably why we always referred to him only as "Jarod;" never his first name, never a nickname.

We'd all seen the beheading videos, I would bet. They lurked down deep in the recesses of our minds. But we all wanted to keep them there, and we didn't need Jarod to bring them out into the open.

"You got any better news for us, Carl?" Rick asked.

"Well, uh, . . ." he said as he tried to think. I knew he'd die before failing to pass any good scuttlebutt.

"Ah, maybe this? It seems like someone made off with seven million dollars from the Rasheed Bank, and get this, the bank was right next door to one of the Army COPs."

He looked at us with a satisfied expression.

"Seven million smackers? I could do that, just like that movie, Kelly's Heroes," Cpl Dunlop said.

"That's a hell of a lot of money," Jerry added. "Maybe the doggies helped themselves?"

The story wasn't that engrossing, but I think all of us wanted to get our minds off that missing corporal. We were deep into our own plans on how we would pull off a heist and then get the money back to the US when Cherrydick came in.

"Cpl Haddad, there's some girl at the front gate who's asking for you," he said without preamble.

If there was one thing we never expected to hear here in the Sandbox was that there was a girl waiting for any of us. You could have told us that the Martians had landed, and we'd have thought that was more likely.

"Bullshit," came his surprised response.

"Hey, I'm just passing the word."

The rest of us started to whoop and holler.

"Haddad's going to get some!" cried out Steve in a falsetto, sing-song voice.

"Who is the girl?" Rick asked.

"I don't know. But she said she's the sister of someone you know. That cook, I think, from the DFAC."

That shut us up immediately. This had something to do with Umar.

"Get battled up!" Rick barked up, all serious.

The entire squad threw on our gear, and in a few moments, we were ready to move.

"Pacman, go tell Cpl Mays or SSgt White what's happening. The rest of us, don't do anything stupid. Let's just find out what she wants."

We followed Rick out and moved on down to the gate. As we came up, one of the Marines on guard told the rest of us to hold back, then motioned Rick forward. We watched Rick as he went to the outside of the gate. If this was a ruse of some sort, he would be an easy target of a sniper.

Sitting down on the ground was a fully burkaed, chadored, or whatever they called it, woman. She stood up, hands wringing in front of her and she spoke to Rick. We could see Rick asking her to repeat herself. It seemed like he understood, because he called out to the sergeant of the guard and evidently got an OK as he looked back and called out for me.

"Zach, get up here!"

I always felt a little exposed when I passed through the gate, but this time, I felt it even more. I had the squad just inside the gate and the Marines on security there, but really, it was just Rick and me and a lot of Iraqis out there.

"There's no interpreter here now. He's taking a shit," he told me as I came up before turning back to the girl.

"Tell him again, just like you told me," he told her.

The girls voice was clear through her veil, "Umar brother me. Brother, mother, grenade. Umar money for doster. No money Umar."

It took me a moment to realize she meant "doctor," not "doster." The girl had memorized what she was saying.

"Umar die."

My hear fell. He was dead?

"Umar doster," she said earnestly.

I could see she was trembling. She was scared out of her mind, whether that was because of us or because she was scared to be seen with us, I didn't know. But if she was saying he needed a doctor, then he was still alive.

"Is Umar alive?" I asked.

"Umar, doster," she said again.

"Where is he?" Rick asked.

"Umar, doster."

I reached out and pointed, swinging my hand around, while asking "Umar?"

She seemed to grasp my meaning. She turned to point down one of the roads leading to the gate.

"Umar."

There was a beat up white sedan at the corner. It had to be forty years old. Crouching beside it was an old man. He saw us looking, then raised a hand and waved.

"Umar's in that car," I said, grabbing Rick's arm. "I'm sure of it."

"I think you're right."

He turned to the sergeant of the guard who was watching us intently.

"We need to get that vehicle in here. Can I motion it forward?"

"Not going to happen," the sergeant said.

I wanted to scream out, but he was right. Vehicles did come in and out of the Point, but they were escorted to us and searched. A beat-up old car was common platform for a VIED, and even if this girl was really Umar's sister, she could be being forced to be an accomplice in an attack.

"Can we go out there?" he asked.

"You need to get permission first," he said.

"Look, that's Umar out there, you know him, right? From the DFAC?"

"Of course I know him." He hesitated, then said, "Look, this might be my ass, but you take two more guys, then get over and get back. If that's really Umar, then carry him back here. He's cleared, so we can let him in, but not the girl."

"Fair enough," Rick said.

"La'Ron, Steve, get out here. The rest of you cover us."

Steve Jenner was a pretty big guy, so he could help carry Umar. La'Ron was not a big guy, and for a moment, I wondered why Rick had picked him. But then I realized that PFC or not, La'Ron was one of the coolest Marines we had when the shit hit the fan. Nothing fazed him.

"OK, let's go," he told us.

By force of habit, we disbursed as we walked across the open area in front of the gate, our formation only spoiled by the robed girls walking in the middle of us. Thirty seconds later, we reached the car. The old man stepped back, and for a moment, I thought that was the signal for the car to explode. But he was only afraid.

I looked in the back seat, and Umar was lying down on it. He wasn't moving. I opened the door, mindless of booby traps, and felt for a pulse. They guy was burning up, his skin hot and dry. His pulse was febrile and weak. As I leaned over to check his eyes, I was almost overcome with the smell of rotted flesh. His shirt was discolored, and I could see the seeping stains of puss.

"We've got to get out of here, Zach," Rick said urgently, reminding me that I could not sit and go through my entire assessment out here in Indian country.

"Steve, give me a hand," I said, and the two of us pulled Umar out of the car. Steve hoisted Umar on his shoulder, and we high-tailed it back to the gate. I think I actually sighed with relief as we made it through.

Just inside the final barrier, we laid him down on the deck so I could get a good look at him. Even without a full assessment, I could see he was about gone. His eyes were slightly open, but rolled back. His breath was extremely shallow and quick. I pulled back his shirt, and over his belly was a wad of rags acting as a bandage. They were soaked with foul-smelling fluid. Two of the Marines who were standing beside me watching stepped back, covering their noses.

The missing interpreter came through the barriers where he had gone to talk to Umar's sister.

"That is the sister. She says someone threw a grenade into their house. The mother and Umar were hit, but they have little money. They only have enough to pay doctor for mother. Umar never no went to doctor."

"When did that happen? I need to know how long ago," I asked as I peeled back the makeshift bandages.

I couldn't even tell how many pieces of shrapnel had hit him. His entire belly and groin were swollen and leaking serum. It was pretty obvious that infection had set in hard, and he had a very short time left.

"Four days ago, that was when," the interpreter said.

He looked concerned, probably considering that he could be a target too for working for us. If a cook was punished, how much worse would it be for an interpreter?

"Rick, he's pretty bad off. We need to get him to Charlie Med, and like now. We can't wait."

"OK, you heard him. We're not going to wait for a vehicle. We're going to carry him to the boat basin and across the river. John, can you go clear this with the powers-that-be?" he asked Cpl Choi.

We picked him up as Cpl Choi took off at a run. We were hurrying, but Umar was beyond feeling the jarring we were wracking on him. An incoming mortar round landed up ahead, something that happened a number of times a day, but I barely noticed. Half-way to the basin, Gunny Tora and Cpl Choi drove up in a hummer, and we put Umar on the hood. I sat there with him as we drove to the river.

One of the India Marines had already started the engine on one of the boats. We loaded Umar on the hood, then Rick and I got in as well as we took off across the river.

Word had been passed at Camp Ramadi, to. An ambulance was there waiting for us, and five minutes later, we were taking him into the Charlie Med ER. One of the Army doctors immediately took charge, and he was put up on an examining table.

"When was this man wounded?" a voice asked behind me.

I turned to look. A major was there wearing the collar tab of what was probably the Army version of the medical service corps. She wasn't a doctor, but she would be on the admin side of care.

"He was wounded four days ago, ma'am," I said.

"Stop it, stop it!" she shouted at the medical team who had just stripped Umar of his clothes.

Everyone turned to look at her.

"According to our new orders, Iraqi civilian nationals can only be admitted if their injury was suffered within 24 hours. Anything over that, and they need to get care in an Iraqi hospital."

She had taken several steps forward as she was speaking until she was right up against the table.

"But he works for us! They tried to kill him because of that!" I shouted out.

"It makes no difference," she said over her shoulder. To the rest, she ordered, "Prepare him for transport."

The gathered team looked at her, motionless. I couldn't believe they were going to send Umar away, to send him to his death.

After an eternity, the doctor turned back to Umar and said, "Let's prep him for surgery. Someone get Doctor Hawkins."

"Captain Vance," the major said with emphasis on the *captain*, "I don't believe you heard me. You will not treat this man.

"I heard you, *Major* Stallings, but you see, once I've started treatment, and as a *physician*, I am not allowed to stop life-saving measure. It's in my oath, you know."

"It doesn't look to me that you've started any treatment. This man will be transferred," she said, steel in her voice.

Dr. Vance reached over and took one of the swabbing brushed used to sterilize large areas of skin, and with one stroke, made a large, brown-colored swath across Umar's chest.

"You were saying. Major?"

She just stood there watching as the team drew blood and got Umar ready for surgery.

"You'll hear from the colonel about this," she said before wheeling and stomping out.

I watched as IV's were put in and Umar was prepared. Dr. Hawkins, the same guy who did my surgery, came in and listened intently as he was brief by the Army doc. The surgery team took over and wheeled Umar out.

"Will he make it?" I asked the doctor as he took off his gloves.

"Don't know. That infection was pretty advanced. But Hawk's a good surgeon, so he might pull through. Another hour or so, though, and I think he'd be gone. At least now, he's got a fighting chance."

"Well thanks. He's sort of a mascot to the Marines in the battalion."

"No thanks necessary. We aim to please."

He started to walk past me when I stopped him.

106

"Is that really part of the Hippocratic Oath? That not being able to stop treatment?"

"Ah, who the hell knows? It was all in Ancient Greek, and they told us about the oath all the way back in pre-med. But she doesn't know, that's for damn sure, and I wasn't going to let some admin pogue tell me what to do in my ER."

Jonathan P. Brazee

Chapter 20

Ramadi General Hospital
July 5, 2006

I wanted to work in a hospital, so I thought it ironic that here I was in one, even if I had just helped take it.

Ramadi General Hospital was a large complex, seven stories high, with about 250 beds. It had been considered off limits at first, but Al Qaeda had been not only using it to treat their own wounded, but they had been using the roof as a sniper nest from where they could fire on us. The last straw was when several Iraqi policemen who were wounded and taken there for treatment were found beheaded. Medical facility or not, it was now officially a target.

This was a battalion objective with two companies in the attack. Only, there wasn't much of an attack. The insurgents melted away before we got there. We found a mostly empty building with only a few patients and very little staff.

We slowly cleared the building. I was more interested in the layout and the equipment than in fighting. I had to keep reminding myself to keep up my level of concentration.

Once we realized that Al Qaeda was not going to contest the building, the Iraqi police, in their light blue shirts and black helmets, stormed in, probably anxious to show that they were on the job.

"Yea, show up now, you stupid hajiis," Jarod said as yet another group of IPs stuck their heads in the ward we were clearing, then disappeared.

"Steady, there," said Cpl Mays. "Remember what the lieutenant said about insulting our illustrious allies. If they want to take credit for this, just let them."

We broke open lockers, medicine chests, anything that might be holding weapons. We never found anything, but First Platoon found a pretty big haul of IED triggering devices hidden in the overhead of one of the offices.

All in all, it hadn't been a bad day. We had expected the fight to be pretty fierce, and while we didn't take it to the insurgents, neither had we suffered any casualties. I'd take that as a win.

Chapter 21

Ramadi
July 12, 2006

I tried to lean forward, anything to change the position of my back. I think I carried everything I owned when we were dismounts. Not only did I have the full combat load of every Marine, but I had all my medical gear as well. Kneeling at the side of the road was a great breather, but I knew the signal to get up and move out again would come any minute.

I looked over at the ISF jundiis on the other side of the road. They didn't carry even half of the gear we did. SSgt White said that was because they were still in training, but this was OJT, and we were getting hit on almost every patrol now. If they could carry less, I wondered why we couldn't.

Patrolling with the ISF was not our favorite thing to do. The jundiis were better than they used to be, according to some of the older salts, but still, they were not up to snuff, and not many had the will to fight. One whole battalion had to be sent back to Baghdad after an IED gave one of their hummers a flat tire—no one was even hurt. But they refused to patrol after that happened, and the BCT commander fired them, just like that.

Just a few years ago, many of them were in Saddam's army, and they were fighting us. Most of the Marines thought that some of them still were fighting us. Just a week ago, an ISF soldier opened up on his MiTT, killing an Army captain and an NCO. Shot them both dead.

I looked up ahead where the senior MiTT member, Gunny Sandoval, was conferring with the lieutenant on our route. That was one job I don't think I'd want. He and SSgt Bronstein were eating, sleeping, and fighting with the ISF. They were commanded by a major, I think, and there were more members of the team, but when we went out with the ISF, it was usually with only one or two Americans with them. No, the Military Transition Team would not be my top choice, even if the word "transition" hinted that we Americans would be getting out of this place. Other countries, like Spain, were pulling out. Only the Brits and the Poles were really sticking around in any numbers, from what I'd heard.

We'd been going out in the daylight more often lately. When mounted, daylight was good because we could see IEDs better. But when dismounted, we liked the darkness. The common saying back at the Point was "We own the night." In the daylight, we knew we were under constant observation: sniper fire, mortars, and rockets were a constant threat.

Thinking of mortars made me look up again. We didn't like to stop while out on patrol. That gave them time to fire off a few rounds at us. I hoped the lieutenant figured out what was going on so we could get moving again.

But back to the ISF, they didn't like the night. So we went out more often on these joint patrols in the daytime, under observation, and in 100 degree-plus temperatures.

The lieutenant made his decision, and the signal to get up was given. I took another sip of water from my CamelBak and struggled to my feet. I was OK when already up, but getting up was sometimes a bitch.

This patrol was to investigate a possible IED factory. We'd been given intelligence on where it was. Weapons platoon, or the Combined Action Platoon, as they were now officially designated (even if we usually used the old term out of habit), had set up checkpoints 200 meters beyond our target. They would be the blocking force.

Up ahead, I could see the intersection that was one of our own route checkpoints. We had to cross this open area first, and then another 150 meters or so was our objective.

Any open area was a hazard. I knew we had sniper overwatch, but they had snipers, too, and ever since the Chechnyan snipers had joined them, they were getting much more effective.

At the intersection, the security element oriented down both directions of the perpendicular road, the one we were crossing. Then, two at a time, we sprinted across. I was maybe the tenth American to cross, but still, I felt the unseen crosshairs of some Al Qaeda sniper aiming in on me.

Actually, it didn't take very long, and all the Americans and jundiis were across and to the other side. We were now pretty close to our staging area, from where we would launch into the attack.

Up ahead, 15 or 20 pigeons took flight.

La'Ron looked at me and pointed at the birds, shrugging his shoulders.

The pigeons were probably a signal that we were getting close. If there were insurgents at the IED factory, they would either scatter or settle in for a serious fight. This being Ramadi, it would probably be the fight.

I'd only taken a couple of more steps before all hell broke loose. Machine gun fire opened up in front of us, the bright green tracers of the enemy making arcs over our heads. I jumped over the wall I'd been walking next to, falling in a heap in a courtyard. La'Ron was right behind me. We moved forward to the gate, then pushed it open a crack, La'Ron high and me low, weapons out and looking for a target.

Behind us and down the road from where we'd already been, another machine gun let loose. I scanned the rooftops, looking for targets.

Most of the Marines had crashed into homes and courtyards when the machine gun opened up. I could hear the lieutenant in the next courtyard over yelling on the radio for support.

The ISF soldiers, though, had merely hit the deck up against the street side of the walls in front of the homes. Several of them had jumped into the narrow canals that ran in front of the walls, the small open sewers filled with septic fluid and waste.

Across the street, just in front of the lead jundii, was a narrow alley. We tended to avoid them. They looked inviting, but the bad guys knew that. No, it was better to make our own paths.

Rounds were clipping all the buildings around us, sending chips of mortar and cinder block down on us. The muzzles of the guns weren't depressed enough to hit us, which meant either these gunners were extremely poor marksmen, or there was another game afoot. If they were merely holding us in place, that might mean that we had incoming. But mortars didn't do much against prone Marines.

One of the ISF soldiers pointed from his position to the alley, turning his head to call out to his fellow soldiers.

"Don't do it," La'Ron muttered. "Keep it cool."

But a decision had been made. En mass, seven or eight jundiis jumped up and ran for the alley. Gunny Sandoval, who had been prone with them, jumped up, screaming something in Arabic. I heard the English word "No!" in the mix, so I got the drift.

He ran forward, grabbing one soldier by the collar and throwing him backwards on his ass onto the street. He kept running, reaching out for another just as he disappeared into the alley.

The explosion was muffled, but it sent plumes of smoke coming out. I didn't hesitate. I pushed open the gate and ran as fast as I could for the alley. I expected the machine gunners to focus on actually hitting us now that their trap had been sprung, but the guns had gone silent. They gunners were probably making their escape.

Regardless, as I got to the alley, I held up, back against the street wall. SSgt Bronstein and one of the ISF soldiers hit the wall opposite of me. The staff sergeant said something in Arabic, and the two turned and dashed into the still smoking alley. I waited about five seconds, then I went in, too.

The alley was only about eight or maybe nine feet across, and the smoke from the explosion was slowly drifting up. As the viz cleared, I could see the havoc caused by the blast.

It looked like several of the Iraqis had already gotten prone, and that might have saved them. Their moans, at least, told me that they were still alive. Others, though, weren't so lucky. My attention was caught for a moment on an intact arm, hanging eight feet up from the tattered remains of a cloth covering, the kind the shopkeepers used to give their storefront shade. From the uniform sleeve that still covered it, I knew it was an ISF arm.

Right at my feet were two bodies. Gunny Sandoval's torso seemed mostly intact, but his legs and one arm were gone. His head was almost gone, the gruesome angle evidence that his neck and been broken clear through. Next to him was a jundii, well, the top half of one, probably the guy he'd been trying to stop. He should have listened to the gunny.

"What do we have, Zach?" HM2 Sylvester asked as he ran into the alley.

I just pointed at the gunny. I hadn't known him that well, but still, this Marine had just died trying to save ISF soldiers. Iraqis.

"Treat the living," Sylvester said as he knelt next to one of the moaning jundiis.

I shook my head, but knelt as well, starting my assessment.

Of the eight men who had entered the alley, including the gunny, five were KIA. Three were WIA, one critical.

After the explosion, Weapons Platoon had shifted missions and hit the target. They blasted down the doors of one very surprised, frightened, and innocent family. The "intel" had all been part of the ambush.

We got the wounded out of there. I watched them leave, then started to walk back across the street. An Iraqi ISF soldier stood there, looking at me. It took me a moment, but then I recognized him. He was the one that Gunny Sandoval had pulled back, the one the gunny had saved.

He looked up at me with pleading eyes, as if he wanted to say something.

I didn't give him a chance. I shouldered past him, knocking him back as I went.

Chapter 22

Ramadi
July 18, 2006

We were back on fly bait duty, but this time, there we were only four hummers, just our squad. Oh, the rest of the platoon was at one of the Army COPs, just a few blocks away, ready to react. But for the moment, we were out there all alone.

When we first started this tactic, the insurgents were easily goaded into attacking us. But now, after being spanked hard time and time again, they were more reluctant to come out and play with us. Not that I disagreed with their thinking, but the fact was that we now had to offer up a juicier target—us.

The lieutenant was with us along with a captain, the battalion Air Officer. So at least it wasn't just Cpl Mays and us sitting out here in Indian country on our lonesome.

"Think they're coming?" Steve Jenner asked for the umpteenth time.

"They'll come if they come," Cpl Choi answered with the resigned tone that a father might have after listening to his kids keep asking "Are we there yet?"

There was probably only a year or two's difference between the corporal and Jenner, but there was a world of difference in their level of maturity.

"Well, I wish they'd just get it over with," Steve muttered as he clicked his safety off and back on again, a nervous tic that he had recently begun to display.

I understood Steve's anxiety. Things had been heating up, and the battalion was suffering more casualties. There wasn't a day that Marines weren't in the shit, and the pressure was building up. Couple that with a shifting schedule of night patrols, day patrols, security duty, and what have you, well, it was beating down on us. I think a few of the guys were at the end of their mental ropes.

The waiting was almost worse than the fighting, though. At least then, we didn't have time to think much. Sitting in the hummer, a piece of fly bait, well, that gave a guy a chance to think, a chance to wonder if the battalion would soon be standing at attention for our own Hero Flight. Wondering where our photo would go up on the battalion CP's Hero Wall.

Time dragged on. Nothing stirred in the heat until a pack of feral dogs came trotting by, stopping to nose our hummers, undoubtedly wondering if we were fair game. We were taught in our classes back at Lejeune that the Muslims thought dogs were unclean. If these were a reasonable sample of Iraqi dogs, then I could understand that. The feral dogs were mangy, dirty mutts. But they would take you down if they could. No Marine or soldier had been killed by a pack, despite rumors to the contrary, but several packs had attacked in the past, once just a month ago. They had been driven off with a few bursts of fire, but the fact that they would take on armed men was always at the back of each man's mind.

The dogs, at some unseen command, suddenly turned and trotted off. As they disappeared from sight, we were alone once again. Nothing stirred. It was even too hot for the flies. I pulled at the edge of my gloves, trying to get some air in. I'm not sure why I bothered, though. The air around me was probably the same temperature as my skin inside the gloves.

Even though we were waiting for it, when the double boom of the RPG came, it came as a shock. RPGs always had two booms. The first was as it was fired and the second, a moment or so later as it hit, sending its molten plasma and shrapnel into whatever it struck. I looked ahead to see if that plasma had gone into one of our hummers as our gunners opened up on a building about 50 meters down the street.

Our hummers were intact. The cloud of smoke on the building just beyond Rick's hummer showed me that the RPG gunner had hit too high. This meant he was probably up high in the building we were now taking under fire. When firing down, gravity had less effect on a projectile, so this was a common mistake. This time, that mistake might have save Rick, his team, and the lieutenant.

One of our hummers had been mounted with a MK19 grenade launcher, and the gunner from Weapons Company attached to us started launching grenade after grenade at our target. With the .50 cals, we were peppering the building, but still fire was coming back at us. There was another boom, and I could see the rocket coming at us. It hit the dirt right in front of us and skipped past, less than a meter from the front of our hummer. There was an almost immediate boom in back of us, and we were showered with broken plaster. La'Ron cried out in anger, but he kept pumping out rounds.

We had three .50 cals and one Mk19 in the attack, but as Marines, we wanted to bring more to the party. I kept craning my neck up, waiting.

I never saw the bomb, but I felt the concussion as the building with the insurgents just disappeared. One huge blast, an equally huge fountain of flame and smoke, and a shower of debris that had La'Ron ducking down for cover, and where there had been a seven-story building was now a half-story pile of rubble.

"That was your boys, there, Doc. Freaking awesome," Cpl Choi turned to me and said.

"Fly Navy!" I said, the best I could come up with despite hours trying to come up with an Arnold-like one-liner. So *The Terminator* I wasn't.

The building was gone. Zippo. Nada. But that wasn't enough. A long, prolonged burst of fire rained down from above like a swarm of huge, angry mutant wasps. No one could have survived that initial blast, but the big C-130 gunship loitering overhead wasn't taking any chances. As soon as the Navy F-18 hit the building with its bomb, the Air Force plane rushed in for its turn. It just slammed the rubble with its 25 mm gatling cannon, making little pebbles out of big chunks of concrete.

After the C-130 left the station and the dust cleared, the order came to move out. Dunlop's hummer pulled out first, followed by the rest. We drove right past the demolished building as we made our way back to the COP to link up with the rest of the platoon. Wisps of smoke and dust were floating up in the still air. There was a bitter smell of some chemical residue from the bomb, not overpowering, but there none-the-less, mixed up with the smell of pulverized concrete. Not for the first time, I was glad I was part of the US forces and not facing them.

Chapter 23

Hurricane Point
July 23, 2006

"Hey, you hear about that Marine from Fallujah who got captured?" Pacman asked as he came into our SWA.

I felt my heart drop. This wouldn't be good.

"He fought off the insurgents and got away. I just heard it at the company CP."

"No shit?" Rob Runolfson asked, swinging his legs around to sit up on his rack.

The rest of us were making similar expressions of surprise.

"Yea, they were like, going to cut off his head, you know, like in those videos. But he and some British soldier went hand-to-hand and messed them up good."

I was shocked, to be honest. But overriding that shock was a thrill that someone had managed to fight back. My morale shot straight up; everyone else's had too, if the excited chatter that greeted the news was any indication. We'd just been sitting around waiting, so this gave us something to talk about.

The platoon was the battalion Quick Reaction Force for the day. This could mean that we'd be in camp all day. But if things went to form, we could be called out not only once, but several times. Some guys liked being the QRF. We sat around in our full battle gear, but there wasn't usually humping involved. If we went out, we went out fast and mounted. For me, though, I never really liked it much. The waiting sucked, but more to the point, if we did go out, it was because someone was in a shit sandwich, a sandwich where we would soon be.

Some of us had been dozing, backs on the racks, booted feet on the deck, but this had gotten everyone's attention. We wondered how that Marine had managed to do it, and that led wondering what we'd do if we were captured. Jerry Scanlon flat out said that if any of us saw him being carried off by the ragheads, we should just shoot him right then and there.

The talk started to peter out as our thoughts turned inward. Being captured by the insurgents was a fear always floating around in the back of our minds.

Cy Pierce broke that train of thought. "Hey, Jenns, what day are we at?"

"Oh shit, I forgot!" Steve answered, jumping up to get to his locker.

"Hey man, you can't go forgetting that," La'Ron called out. "Thems bad juju, man. You miss a day, and maybe we have to stay a day longer."

Steve Jenner had a shortimer's calendar, but one that went above and beyond. The background of the calendar was a photo of his girlfriend. Covering the photo were small stickers, each with a number on it. There had been 190 stickers, and a good portion of them had been removed, one at a time as each day went by. Enough had been removed to show that Corrine was naked and was holding a sign saying "Come home to this, Stevie," with an arrow pointing down at her crotch, and she was hot. No, not hot, but smoking hot.

To say she was completely naked, though, was only conjecture. The remaining stickers were strategically placed around her tits and pussy. By careful examination, it looked like she was topless, but the debate was whether a g-string hid her goods.

Steve was completely at ease with sharing his calendar with us. I couldn't imagine doing that with Amy. She had given me a rather revealing photo before I left, but I had that secured and would never show that to anyone. Steve, though, didn't mind when we ogled Corrine.

He brought out the precious calendar, then scanned it for the day's sticker. Cy, Bret, and La'Ron crowded around him as he found it, then pulled it off.

"Ah, man," Jarod exclaimed.

I wanted to get up to see, but I didn't want to act like I was drooling over his girlfriend, me a married man and all.

"Just a little side titty," Jarod said as he sat back down. "I want to see the good stuff."

"You might want to see it," Steve said as he put the calendar back in his locker, "but in two months, I'll be doing more than that!"

La'Ron held up a fist, and Steve obliged with a bump.

I know it takes all kinds, and I know we had forged a bond of brotherhood, but Steve's openness about his girlfriend was something I couldn't get my head around. That didn't stop me from taking a look, though, on occasion, and watching the slow, seven-month strip-tease.

I was sitting on Rick's rack as mine was a top bunk. I leaned back, keeping my booted feet off the rack and on the deck. With Steve's ritual, I started thinking about Amy. I missed her pretty badly, and I wanted to see my son. But I was also a bit apprehensive about seeing them again. How would I fit in? Would Tyson even remember me?

I was lost in my thoughts when the alert came through. A sniper team was in trouble, and we had to go extract them. Within moments, we were up and out by the hummers. We were getting mentally prepared while the lieutenant was getting his orders. We had to focus. A rocket or mortar landed inside the camp about 200 meters away or so, but this was so commonplace that we didn't react. If someone was hurt by that rocket, then others would take care of it. We had our own mission, and at least two Marines were depending on us.

The lieutenant joined us in about five minutes, and he took another two or three minutes to give us our op order. For normal missions, we took a lot longer going over details. But as the QRF, any time wasted could make a difference. We mostly used SOPs, adjusting them as necessary.

The sniper team was on the roof of one of the buildings a couple of hundred meters from the government center. They'd called in being under attack, and we knew at least one of them had been hurt. It was up to us to get to them.

Within moments, we were rolling. Our squad was the assault element. We would fight our way up to them if they could not come down. I took out my magazine, checked the rounds, and re-seated it.

We barreled down Michigan. We knew that this could be a trap, that the road could be mined now. But Michigan was kept pretty clear, and by going fast, we could make it more difficult for any RPG gunners, or even mess up the timing of remote-controlled IEDs.

We made it to the rallying point without incident, piling out of the hummers. Third Squad was the security element, and they secured the area. First was technically the support element, but as usual, we tended to go into a hybrid organization, almost as if we had two assault elements. It may not be by the book, but we found that it tended to work better for house-clearing.

I looked up to where a Cobra was circling. I overheard enough to know that the roof was clear, but there was a blood trail leading back inside. The Cobra would remain on station until we had the team back.

The familiar calls of "Coming in," "Clear," and "Move" were soon ringing out as I followed my stack into the building. This was routine, and I was moving almost by rote memory. That was dangerous, though. As the sign at the Point said, "Complacency kills!"

The ground floor of the building was empty. That didn't mean anything, though. If the building was truly empty, wouldn't the sniper team make it down to meet us? Champ Dykstra kept trying to raise them, but there was no response.

Rick's team started to move up the first flight of stairs. Stairs were pretty vulnerable places for us. We couldn't mass firepower, and we were fighting gravity. Pacman had the point, Jerry Scanlon was next with the SAW, then Rick and Jarod. I followed them, senses on high alert. I was filtering out the shouts of clearing, striving to hear anything out of the ordinary.

There was a light thudding sound of something hitting the stairs. Something bounced off Pacman's shoulder, then started to curve down towards us.

I shouted "Frag!" as I felt more than saw Marines hitting the deck. Gunfire erupted from above us, stitching the wall beside Pacman. I looked up and clear as day, I saw the grenade come at me as if in slow motion. It was an American grenade, I noted, almost as if it was of no consequence. A grenade, though, in this confined ladderwell would have pretty grave consequences.

About a foot from my head, Rick's arm shot out, cleanly fielding the grenade. He stepped up, ignoring the firing coming from above, and by leaning over, got the angle he wanted and threw the grenade back up the stairs. Throwing a grenade up a stairs was something else that could have grave consequences. Grenades thrown up stairs usually came back down.

This time, whether due to Rick's golden arm or by pure luck, the grenade did not come back down. It exploded above us.

"Go, go go!" Rick shouted, echoed by Cpl Mays behind me.

We were up the stairs and to the next floor in seconds. A dead insurgent was at the top of the stairs, his body riddled with shrapnel. In front of us was another floor that had to be cleared. Another flight of stairs led to the top floor of the building.

Rick's team held the landing as Cpl Mays and Cpl Choi's team made it up the stairs. The squad leader was just telling Cpl Choi to start clearing the floor when the fire from at least three or four weapons opened up from above us. I caught a glimpse of an AK being held out over the ladderwell, blindly firing down at us. I fired at the hands. I don't know if I hit them, but the AK was pulled back. Another grenade came up over the railing and floated down to us.

"Frag" and "Grenade" rang out as we dove to get out of the way. Once again, Rick decided to play center field. Instead of diving, he stepped forward, fielded the grenade, and with a weird, side arm motion, tossed the grenade back up the ladder and over the rail. We waited a very long moment, and I half expected to see it come back at us, but the explosion rained nothing more than dust and debris down at us.

Immediately, we rushed the ladder, making it up to the top floor, eagerly looking for targets. There was no one there. A door to the roof was open, and the whup-whup of the Cobra outside took on a different tone. Within moments, we could hear the deep chatter of the Cobra's 20 mm gatling opened up.

"Doc, here!" shouted Pacman, pointing to the blood trail leading to one of the rooms. He started to rush forward, but Rick grabbed him. We weren't sure who was in there. It looked like the hajiis bugged out, but they've been known to have suicide fighters willing to die if they could take out one of us at the same time.

Rick positioned his team to provide security down the hallway, and Cpl Dunlop took his team to get ready to enter. I got on his ass, ready to follow him in.

At Cpl Dunlop's signal, Cy shouted "US Marines, coming in left!"

Rob echoed with "Coming in right!"

They moved as one, sweeping into the room. Cpl Dunlop and I followed, almost running up the back of Cy as he had stopped dead. I looked around him and froze.

Two Marines were lying on their backs against the far wall, feet towards the middle of the room. Their heads were detached from their bodies and placed on their chests, facing whomever entered the room. In each mouth was a severed penis and testicles. As one Marine was black and another white, it was clear they had put the other man's penis in each Marine's mouth.

My head started spinning, and I heard retching. I wasn't sure if it was me or not at first. I walked over to the two snipers as it there was something I could do. Almost as from a distance, I noted that one of the Marines had a badly mangled face and shoulder. He had probably been dead before they had cut off his head.

The other Marine had a smashed femur, but from the amount of blood and the spray, I would say he was alive when they did this to him.

"Cpl Dunlop," the lieutenant said, "get your team out and finishing clearing this building."

I hadn't heard him come in, but that wasn't surprising. He looked gray, and he was swallowing hard, but he had taken charge, making sure we did what we had to do.

Jonathan P. Brazee

"Go down to the second floor, Doc, and see if you can help Doc Seychik," he told me.

I figured that he just wanted me to keep busy, but I complied. In somewhat of a daze, I walked down the ladder to see Buster working over a body. I knew that hajii was already dead, so why take the effort? Even if he had been alive, should we save him after what he did to those two Marines?

It wasn't until Buster leaned back in defeat that I saw he wasn't working on the hajii. It was Steve Jenner. I took the last two steps in a bound and rushed up. Buster looked up at me and shook his head. I stood there in shock, then knelt beside him. His flak jacket and blouse had been taken off, exposing his chest. A round had hit him in the jaw, it looked like, then traveled into his neck and down into his chest cavity. I couldn't see an exit wound, but the round had to have mangled his internal organs as it traveled through his body.

With the SAPI plates, the flak jacket can stop most small arms rounds. But this round had come from above, entering his body from the small opening caused by his neck. Steve must have been looking up when he was hit. I thought of the AK I had seen. Had that coward, afraid to show his face, actually managed to blindly shoot and kill Steve?

I pulled the flak jacket closed over his chest.

We had received the news today that a Marine had escaped certain death in an amazing escape. But two other Marines might have paid the price for that, their beheading a stark message that Al Qaeda in Iraq was not about to roll over on us. And as a result, Steve had become the squad's third KIA.

Of the insurgents, there was one killed. The rest got away over the roof, the Cobra not being able to fire until they reached the other building as its 20 mm cannon fire would've gone right through the roof of this building, hitting us as well.

One for three was not an exchange any of us could accept.

Chapter 24

Ramadi
July 26, 2006

The mood within the squad was bleak. We were tired, mentally as well as physically. Losing Steve had affected all of us. When Cpl Morrison had come in to get his effects, we told him that was our job. We gathered up everything, stopping at Corrine's calendar. The regs were that everything would be gathered. But should his family get that? Would he want that? On the other hand, as Rick pointed out, shouldn't Corrine know that he had appreciated her efforts?

In the end, Cy, Steve's best friend, took the calendar, put it in a large envelope, and sealed it. He knew Corrine, and he would make that decision later back at Lejeune.

Steve Potts' Hero Ceremony had been bad enough. But to be blunt, we were new to the Sandbox then, and we hadn't bonded with him to the same degree that we had with Steve Jenner. As with Sgt Butler, we'd gone through a lot with him. Cy wasn't the only one who shed tears during the memorial.

Now we were out on yet one more patrol. We had gone out on a meet and greet during the night, planning to come back before morning. It was now almost 1600 the next day. We had had no food since about midnight, and at that point, all of us were out of water.

Al Qaeda had stepped up the pressure. They were losing Ramadi, and they weren't going to meekly slink away into the desert. They needed a victory to rally the young Iraqis to their cause, men who were getting tired of the foreign Al Qaeda's heavy-handed methods. The local sheiks were starting to align with us, and Al Qaeda needed to turn that tide with some sort of victory over us.

The entire battalion was engaged, each company in the fight. Some general, I forgot who, said that modern warfare was turning into a three-block war. I didn't know what he meant when I was told that, but I learned. I could hear firing around us, I could see aircraft, hear the booms of artillery. But my war was winnowed down to the building Second and Third Squad held, the small soccer field next to us, and the building across it that First Squad held. I knew that we were at one end of a line after joining the rest of the company, but I could not see the others, and our PRR's only let us reach to the other squads. The lieutenant could communicate with the company, of course, but as squads, we couldn't.

Getting to the company had been a bitch in and of itself. It took until about noon. We had to run the last 1,000 meters, and I was carrying about 80 pounds of gear. I had drunk the last of my water as I lay panting on the deck of the pock-marked building that gave us some cover. Four hours later, we had cleared only one more building. A machine gun had opened up on us as First Squad was crossing the soccer field. Amazingly, only one Marine had been hit, and not seriously. But the gun was a threat, and we had called in air support. It was a relief to just sit for a moment and wait for the airedales do their thing.

"Hey Doc, can you check my foot?" Cpl Choi asked me as we waited.

I had checked enough feet during this deployment to last me my lifetime. If I knew anything, it was that I was never going to specialize in podiatry. But in some ways, that might have been my most important task. With the heavy loads we carried and the everlasting heat, the Marines' feet took a beating. And without healthy feet, a Marine couldn't move. Every night, I had the squad take off their socks for an inspection, just letting the jokes about me and my foot fetish roll right off me.

Cpl Choi had taken off his boot and sock. I got up to take a look. A nasty smell hit me as I reached him. The top of the foot was filthy. Dirt and sand had worked their way down inside the boot. He rolled on his stomach and lifted his lower leg, exposing the bottom of his foot.

I recoiled a few inches before taking his foot in my hand for a closer examination. He had a huge ulcer, almost three inches across. I couldn't tell how deep it was. By the smell, I knew it was infected. He needed to get back to the aid station, but that wasn't going to happen.

I just cleaned it the best I could, Cpl Choi never flinching even though I knew it had to hurt like hell. I slathered on an antibiotic gel, then built up some padding and bandaged it in place. He had to gingerly slide his boot back over it. It wasn't optimal, but it would have to do.

"Thanks, Doc. I guess your foot fetish came in handy."

"Yea, right. Just make sure you get to the aid station ASAP," I told him.

"Sure. No problem. I'll just saunter on out there and catch a taxi back."

Jerry Scanlon started to laugh at that, then ended up coughing. He had been moved to Third Team after Steve was killed. Cpl Mays said if anyone else was lost, we'd probably have to go to only two fire teams.

The familiar whup-whup told us that our air had arrived. I could hear the lieutenant talking the pilot into the target. The Cobra lined up, then let lose a salvo of rockets, following up with its 20 mm gatling. An Apache might have more firepower, but the Cobra was no slouch, either. The building from where we'd been taking fire erupted in dust and smoke.

"Get some, Mr. Cobra," La'Ron said as we watched it finish its run and peel off.

The lieutenant got back on the PRR and told Sgt Castanza to come on back. At one end of the soccer field, we knew the road was covered by the insurgents. At the other end, the Cobra had made mincemeat of the building. The quickest way to reunite the platoon was for them to run back across the field, over maybe 40 meters or so of open ground.

We all took positions to cover them, and after a few minutes, the first two men started to run across. Amazingly, the hajii machine gun opened up again from the building adjacent to the one that had been taken out. The two Marines immediately turned and ran back to their building.

The lieutenant immediately got back on his radio and tried to get the Cobra back, but evidently, it was almost out of fuel and we'd have to wait.

I heard the sound of vomiting in the floor above me. I wanted to ignore it, but I got up and made my way up the ladder. HM2 Sylvester was already there, treating Private Jennings, from Third Squad for heat exhaustion. We had three Marines suffering from it already, and without water, more would probably get hit. I made my way back down.

SSgt White saw me come back down and hurried over. He'd been looking for me.

"Doc Cannon, we've got someone down hard in First. They need you there now," he said.

"I didn't see anyone get hit," I said.

"I don't think it's that. It's Castanza. They say it's serious."

"How am I supposed to get there?" I asked, looking out the blasted window to the building across the way.

"Run your fucking ass off!" was his reply.

At first, I thought he was joking. Then I realized he was serious.

"We wouldn't ask you, but it sounds real bad."

I caught the "ask," not "order." I didn't have to go.

The lieutenant came up behind him and asked, "Well?"

I looked around. All the Marines there were watching me, waiting to hear what I said. What I wanted to say was that my first job was to keep safe so I could treat them. I wanted to say that my wife told me not to be a hero. I wanted to say a lot of things.

What I did say was "No problem. I'm good to go."

Did I see relief sweep the platoon sergeant's face?

I knew it had to be me. With Buster out wounded and back at camp, it had to be me or Sylvester. And what I had thought about keeping safe to treat the Marines, well between Sylvester and me, he was more qualified. So I was up.

"Good man, Doc," he said, giving me a slap on the shoulder. "Drop your gear here. Just take your kit. We're going to cover you, but you've got to run like a fucking deer. No fucking zigzag bullshit. No stopping. Just run."

I took one last suck on my CamelBak, as if water had somehow managed to magically form inside of it. It was still empty. I took out most of the crap in my pack, keeping only my medical gear. Clutching my weapon, I considered ditching that, too. I wouldn't be stopping to fire it. But that would make me feel too naked.

When I was ready, I nodded at the platoon sergeant. I walked to where something had taken out a chunk of wall. Steeling myself, I took a few deep breaths, then gave SSgt White a thumbs up I didn't really feel.

On order, Marines opened up in the general direction of the building from which the machine gunner had fired. From our side, I didn't think that anyone had a good angle, but from First Squad's position, they should be able to put rounds on target.

I hesitated only a second, then before I could change my mind, I took off in a mad sprint. I had gotten only about 10 meters when I heard the machine gun open up. I expected to feel lead tear into my body and I tried to do my best Jessie Owens. I knew he had me in his sights, though.

He may have had the bead on me, but he couldn't put rounds on me. Somehow, miraculously, I made it to the other side, diving to the deck of the building there. The First Squad Marines gathered around me and pulled me to my feet.

"Holy shit, Doc! Did you see that!" Ivanski shouted. "It was like, buda buda buda, and the rounds were kicking up in back of you, chasing you all the way to us. You were kick ass!"

PFC Ivan Borisov was excited as he recounted what had happened, his accent growing stronger the more excited he got. Ivanski was one of the two Marines in the platoon who were using service in the Corps to speed up the citizen process.

"It was just like in a movie. Buda, buda, buda," he said, using his hands to mimic firing a machine gun.

I was using his excitement to catch my breath. My hands were trembling, but whether from an adrenaline drain or from dehydration, I wasn't sure.

"OK, where's Sgt Castanza?" I asked after a few moments.

Cpl Cranhover led me to the back where Sgt Castanza lay on the floor, unresponsive. I knelt down and pulled open his eyelids. His eyes were rolled back. I felt for a pulse. His skin was hot and dry, his pulse febrile.

"I need some water!" I shouted.

"Don't have any. Sgt Castanza gave all his away when others ran out. He hasn't drunk since this morning, I think."

I started stripping him. He was burning up, and his battle gear was keeping the heat in.

"Help me," I ordered.

Two Marines rushed to help, LCpl Leslie taking out his K-Bar to get the clothes off quicker. We almost had him naked when Sgt Castanza went into seizure. I jumped on him, holding him down to prevent injury while the seizure lasted.

"Look around," I told Cpl Cranhover. "Get any liquid. We've got to get him cooled down."

I knew what was wrong with him. I just didn't know how bad it was. I pulled out a rectal thermometer and inserted it into him. I waited, then pulled it out. This was an emergency. His core temperature was 109.

"Get on the PRR and tell the lieutenant we need a no-shit immediate casevac," I told the corporal.

"You, you, and you," I said, pointing to three Marines. "I need to you piss on him."

Surprisingly, none of the three hesitated. They unbuttoned their flies and aimed streams of dark piss onto the body of the prone sergeant. The dark color told me they were pretty dehydrated, too.

"Isn't piss hot, too?" asked Doug Apfel, one of the Marines pissing on him.

"Yea, but it's cooler than his temperature, and I need him wet."

I picked up a piece of plywood, shattered in some past firefight, and used it to fan him, trying to accelerate the evaporation process.

"I'll take over that," another Marine said, freeing me up to monitor the sergeant.

"What's with that casevac?" I shouted as I started to feel panic set in.

"They're working on it," Cpl Cranhover shouted back, the PRR held up to his ear.

We took turns emptying our bladders on Sgt Castanza as we waited the 40 minutes for an Army Voodoo Mobile to make it to us. The armored ambulance backed right up into the building, making its own entrance. With rounds pinging off the front of it, we loaded Sgt Castanza in the back and sent it on its way, but not before the crew left ¾ of a case of water.

After another 20 minutes, a Cobra made another run, and this time, it either took out the machine gun or made the gunner withdraw. It wasn't until 2200, almost 24 hours after we left Hurricane Point, that we returned. We had twelve heat casualties in the platoon. Eleven would recover. Sgt Elias Castanza would not. He died 30 minutes after reaching the aid station.

If the insurgents couldn't defeat us, the land itself sure seemed to be trying to.

Chapter 25

Hurricane Point
Sep 8, 2006

"Check out the newbies," Pacman said as he sat down to join us at the table.

We looked around. Our replacement battalion, 1/6, had sent ahead an advance party, and about five of them were getting their food. They looked different from us, but I couldn't really put my finger on it except maybe that they were "clean?"

"Who you calling newbies there, boot?" Cpl Choi asked as he took a bite of mac and cheese.

"Those guys. The ones over there. They just got in, so they're newbies."

"'Those guys are all vets who've been around. This isn't there first time to the dance," he remarked.

"Well yea, maybe, but not like us. I mean, look what we've gone through. Right?"

"See that sergeant over there, the one getting his bug juice?" the corporal asked.

"Yea. So what?"

We all looked over to see who Cpl Choi was pointing out.

"That's Sergeant Matthew Vandermier. My brother was with him with 2/4, right here in Ramadi in 2004. He won the Silver Star, and my brother says it should have been a Navy Cross. He charged a machine gun position when they were pinned down, taking out three hajiis even if he was hit twice."

"Well, OK, but that was one guy. We still have it worse, right?"

"Jeeze, Pacman. You been keeping your head up your ass? You don't listen to what's happened before? 2/4 had 34 killed on their tour here and had over 350 wounded. So how about you take your "newbie" shit and shove that up your ass, too, boot."

Cpl Choi was normally as good natured as they come, but I wondered why he took so much offense. We were all on edge, looking forward to getting out of here, and Pacman should know better than to spout off like that. He, La'Ron, and I were the real newbies here, not even a year in the FMF, but I thought Choi was a little harsh.

"OK, sorry," Pacman said, backing down. "I didn't mean anything by it."

I watched the sergeant as he sat down at his table. Thirty-four KIAs was a huge number. I thought we'd been in the shit, but we weren't even half of that. This close to the end, I hoped we would stay that way.

Chapter 26

Ramadi
Sep 19, 2006

"So, I can get letter from you, right?" Azar asked me yet again.

"I told you yes, but nothing from me is going to help. I'm just an E2. You need something from Captain Wilcox, or the battalion CO."

Azar had been pestering most of us for letters recommending him for asylum in the US. He went on about his uncle getting killed by Al Qaeda, but we got the impression that he just wanted a better life. And now, I couldn't really get away from him, so he kept asking.

"I am not like them," he told me, tilting his head back to indicate the "Shawanie" sitting back in the hummer. "I do what you do. I am the same as a Marine."

He had a point at that. The Shawanies were supposedly some sort of Iraqi Special Forces soldiers, but in reality, they were middle-aged guys in uniform who would rather sit in a hummer than get in a fight. They would come out when called to explain to some woman that we would be taking over her home for an hour, but when fighting started, they usually could be found as far away from the fire as possible.

Azar, on the other hand, never shirked from a fight. I would give him that.

I hoped today wouldn't give him the opportunity to prove himself again. We were on a battalion-wide mission of cordon-and-search, maybe our last full-scale mission before 1/6 took over. The platoon was acting as a blocking force to catch anyone trying to escape to the north. Second squad had the middle road. Third was on the next road to the west, and First was on the one to the east. We had the lieutenant with us and five ISF soldiers. Basically, no one would get past us until the mission was completed.

We'd heard several explosions, but from the sound of them, they were probably just breaching charges. There hadn't been sounds of an out-and-out firefight yet.

I looked around us. We had two hummers blocking most of the road, both with .50 cals at the ready. La'Ron and Pacman were up in the turrets, scanning the avenue of approach from the south.

Jonathan P. Brazee

The lieutenant and Cpl Dykstra were up against the hood of Rick's hummer where the platoon leader had a map laid out in front of him.

The hummers were angled forward, their hoods pointed towards each other. Between the hoods was a wooden barrier, complete with a swing-up gate. This was manned by the ISF soldiers and Cpl Dunlop's team. Second Team had new addition. Cherrydick was with them. The first sergeant had transferred him over to the platoon when First Platoon basically kicked him out. After all this time in the Sandbox, this was only the second time he'd been out in Indian country.

The ISF soldiers seemed to be of better caliber than those who were serving when we arrived. They seemed more focused and more determined. The lieutenant told us that since AQI (he always said "A-Q-I" for Al Qaeda in Iraq instead of just "Al Qaeda" as most of us referred to them) was targeting the sheiks and executing capital punishment at the drop of the hat, more and more tribal men were answering the call.

"Sure Azar, I'll write something up," I told the waiting interpreter.

He thanked me, then wandered over to the lieutenant, probably to bug him about a letter as well. I didn't think having a collection of letters from us would do any good, but then again, what the heck did I know about that stuff?

I wondered when we'd be going home. Every day now, we were expecting to find out the date. If we just knew it, we could get it straight in our minds. A couple of Army units got involuntarily extended in country, and the rumors were starting to crop up that said the same thing might happen to us.

I took another sip from my CamelBak. All of us had nonissue gear, but this was probably my best purchase, something I bought after Sgt Butler had recommended it back at Lejeune. The Marines issued their own version of one, but mine was top-of-the-line. After the heat injuries last month, I kept that thing full. Each hummer had extra water cans, and one of my jobs was now to make sure everyone was topped off.

The sun was beating down on us. Even in September, the daytime temperatures were scorchingly high. I never thought I would welcome getting back to the "cool" North Carolina coast.

My mind started to wander, thinking of my last conversation with Amy on whether she and Tyson would move out to Jacksonville or wait until I had my orders to C-School and a hospital. I sort of zoned out, so when the explosion sounded in front of us, I was caught by surprise. I looked up to see an RPG rocket coming at Cpl Choi's hummer. The fire team leader was just to the side of his vehicle, and he wheeled around at the blast to see what was coming. Almost casually, it seemed to me, he hesitated, then jumped in the air as the rocket passed underneath him, hitting the road and skipping back up again to impact on one of the buildings behind us.

Another blast sounded in front of us, and this rocket was heading toward Rick's hummer. This one didn't miss, flipping the vehicle up and over on its back. I was running before I realized it, the firing barely registering to me. In only a moment, La'Ron opened up in return fire with his .50 cal.

I skidded to a stop in back of the hummer, trusting its bulk to protect me from the rounds that were impacting all around us. Hands reached out of what used to be a window, and I grabbed them, pulling hard. Rick tumbled out, covered with dust and soot, but seemingly unhurt. He scrambled back, and together we looked in. Pacman's legs were right in front of us, his body disappearing out under the turret, so together we tried to pull him back. His legs seemed to give slightly, but I realized that was because they were separating from his torso. He had been crushed when the hummer flipped, and the bulk of the .50 cal hadn't been enough to protect him. Rick started to get another grip to pull again.

"Stop. He's gone," I told him as he looked at me first with confusion, then in shock.

Jarod was jammed up in the back of the cab. I didn't know if hummers could explode like in the movies, but I crawled in, grabbed his wrists, and pulled him out as fast as I could. Rick helped me the last few feet, and I checked Jarod's pulse. It was strong and steady, but he was out cold.

I looked around to see who else was hurt. At the checkpoint, an ISF soldier was down, not moving. I could see the others in back of Cpl Choi's hummer, taking cover while firing down the road. Just in back of me, Cpl Dykstra was crawling up to the hummer as rounds continued to zing around us. I turned and took a step towards him when my foot hit something. To my shock, I realized it was the lieutenant. I had run right past him to look inside the hummer.

He was on his back, his hand up against his throat and chin, trying to stem blood that was welling between his fingers. He looked up at me, his eyes wide as he tried to say something. The lower part of his jaw was shattered, though, so between that and the blood, nothing was coming out. His right foot was under the hummer, trapped between it and the road.

My heart fell as I dropped down beside him.

"Rick, help Dykstra," I said over my shoulder as I assessed the lieutenant.

I pulled his hands back expecting the worst. There was no spurting of bright red blood. His carotids somehow hadn't been compromised. But he still was in desperate shape. The blood was blocking his throat, and I could see mangled flesh and bones. He was choking to death.

I reached in with my hand to clear the airway, but it was like reaching into a bowl of hamburger.

A blast of fire sounded by my ear, making me jump. It was Rick, though, who had reached back in the hummer and pulled out an M16. He sent a couple of three round bursts downrange. I could hear him trying to raise one of the other squads on his PRR, but either the little British radios were having problems again the in the concrete canyons of Ramadi, or they were engaged, too.

There was only one thing I could do for the lieutenant. I reached into my pack, fumbling for the oropharyngeal airway. I thought about using the nasal airway, but with head injuries, we were warned that we could kill a patient by driving one into the brain. I looked at the curved plastic airway in my hand, then back at the lieutenant. For a moment, I hesitated. I'd never inserted an airway in real person before, only a dummy, and all the dangers, the risk of death flashed through my mind. I could kill him right here on the road.

His hand fell weakly to his side. He was barely conscious and would be dead soon, so I had to act. I steeled myself and tried to go through the steps in my mind. I'd checked the airway already. It was a mess. Clear the airway? How was I supposed to do that? It was pretty much blocked, only a tiny bit of air making it in and out. I was supposed to position the airway tilting his head back into the "sniffing" position. That was supposed to enable me to visualize his epiglottis, but with so much blood and so many bone fragments, I couldn't see anything. I just had to go for it.

I took the airway, turning it upside down so the curved tip was up against the roof of his mouth. I pushed until it hit the back of his throat, then with a quick prayer for guidance, twisted it in a 180 and pressed the tube down. It pushed through the mangled flesh and blood, and slid down the throat. I still couldn't see anything, so I had to trust I was in the trachea and not the esophagus. Suddenly the lieutenant's breathing became steadier, and his chest movement more noticeable. By some miracle, I'd done it!

I still had to auscultate the chest and stomach to make sure everything was in place. There were no gurgling sounds in the stomach, so his esophagus was clear, but the sounds in the lungs were not good. He was breathing, but he probably had fluid in his lungs. He could still drown in his own blood.

I tried to pull him back so I could treat that, but his foot was trapped hard under the hummer. He was not going anywhere. I tried to put him up on his side to keep at least one lung clear, but with his foot trapped, his body wanted to lay flat. I had to kneel in back of him, using my body to keep him in position on his side.

Another boom caught my attention, and I looked up to see La'Ron duck down back into his hummer. The RPG round impacted right on the roof of the hummer, the detonation taking the .50 cal right off. The Marines and ISF troops who had been in back of the hummer dropped flat, but it looked like no one had been hit. Anyone standing would have had his head taken off. A moment later, La'Ron popped out of the rear door and joined them.

Cpl Mays shouted over from the other hummer, "Get on the company net and let them know we need help!"

"You've got it, Zach. I'm a little busy here," Rick said, leaning around the hummer to fire. He popped his empty magazine out and slammed home another.

I leaned back, trying to keep the lieutenant in position while I grabbed the handset of the radio Cpl Dystra still had strapped to his back. I wasn't sure how to use it. I was used to the small PRRs. Still I had to figure it was already on the right frequency.

I keyed the handset and said, "Uh, Banger, this is Banger One-Two." I waited, hearing nothing in response. "Oh, over," I answered. Still nothing. Then I remembered to release the transmit button.

"Banger One-Two, this is Banger. What is your situation, over?"

Oh, yea, situation. What was the acronym? SMEAC? Situation, Mission, E for something. A for Action? I was confused.

"Um, Banger, we're under attack. We're pinned down, . . . oh, over," I transmitted.

"Banger One-Two, put Banger One-Actual on, over," the operator on the other side said.

"Banger, the actual is not available. He is WIA, and we need an immediate casevac. We have WIA and KIA here."

There was a pause on the other end, then a new voice came on.

"Banger One-One, this is Banger Actual. Can you clearly tell me what's happening? What is your situation?"

135

"Banger Actual, we have at least two KIA. We've got another two or three WIA and ineffective. We're pinned down, and there are maybe, wait one, . . ." I transmitted, before leaning over the lieutenant to take a glance down the street as if the insurgents were about to stand up and be counted.

It was a pretty dumb move. Whether by chance or by skill, a round hit the radio handset, knocking it out of my hand.

"Son of a bitch!" I shouted, jumping back over the lieutenant.

I shook my hand, only stopping when blood splashed up in my face. I looked at my hand. I thought the round had only hit the handset. I was wrong. The top of my little finger, from about the nail bed on up, was gone.

I stared at it curiously. It was not registering. Holding my hand up, I reached into my pack and brought out a bandage, wrapping it tightly around the tip of my finger.

"You OK there, Zach?" Rick asked.

"Sure. Good to go," I answered, despite feeling a little dizzy.

"You got any extra mags?" he asked me.

"Yea, come get them."

He scooted over, taking four mags from me, leaving me with the full mag still in my weapon and one other.

Cpl Mays called out from where he was with the others, "Get on your PRR!"

Rick shrugged his shoulders, holding up an empty hand.

"We've got to get under cover," the squad leader called out. "We're going to get off the road and into the building over here. Can you make it over?"

It was only about 10 meters to the others, but it was probably five to the courtyard directly abreast of us.

"I've got three to carry and only two of us. We'll take this side. You get in that building over there."

Cpl Mays looked back and forth at each building. He was obviously torn, but he knew that made sense, even if it would be splitting his squad. First squad would be on the other side of the block, so he must have figured we could link up with them.

"OK. Wait for the SAWs and M203 to open up, then move it."

He huddled with the other Marines and the ISF troops giving instructions. The firing from the insurgents had slackened but we all knew they were still out there.

"OK, I'll take Jarod first, then come back for Dykstra. You be ready with the lieutenant," Rick told me.

I looked down at the lieutenant. He wasn't going anywhere, until we could move the hummer off of him. I didn't tell Rick that.

Cpl Mays shouted at us to get ready, then Jerry Scanlon and Cy Pierce jumped out with their SAWs while Rob Runolfson put a 203 round downrange, then opened up his breach, rammed another grenade home, and fired that one, too. At the first burst from the SAWs, the other five Marines and four ISF soldiers made a dash for the building, Cpl Choi slamming himself into the gate. Amazingly, it burst open, getting all of them off the road and out of the line of fire.

At the same time, Rick picked up Jarod, dashing across to the house and to the wall, pushing Jarod up and over before dashing back to me.

The SAWs stopped firing, and the three remaining Marines made their dash as well. The Iraqis were expecting it, and they opened up. I thought I heard a shot from up high and in back of me, and the firing seemed to cut in half, but I couldn't be sure of that. What I was sure of was seeing Jerry go down. Cy stopped, came back through the fire, and grabbed Jerry by his deuce gear, dragging him until he got in the courtyard and under cover.

I started to get up to go over there, but that would probably kill the lieutenant, and I hadn't heard the call of "Corpsman up!" That meant either he was OK or dead.

"Zach, pick up the lieutenant and follow me."

I just shook my head.

"I'm serous, come on!" he said.

"Can't. He's trapped," I told him, pointing his foot.

Rick stepped up, looking at the foot under the hummer. He squatted, grabbed the vehicle and strained. It didn't budge. He scootched back, thinking.

"Look, he's stuck here for now either way. You come with me, and when we've got help, we'll come get him. We can cover him better from over there, anyway."

"Can't do that either," I said. His lungs are filling with blood. If we lay him flat, he'll die. I've got to keep him on his side."

"Well, let's prop him up, then."

"Any movement, he falls flat. And he's gone. Look, I've got the hummer here. They can't hit me. You go get help, and I'll just wait here with him. "

I looked down at the ashen platoon commander. He was struggling for breath, even with the airway bypassing his mangled face and neck. I didn't think he was going to make it.

I think Rick came to the same conclusion.

"Look, as the senior Marine here, I'm ordering you to come with me. Jarod and Dysktra here need your help, and you can do them some good."

"Sorry, Rick, but you know I'm not in your chain of command. I'm staying."

"OK, then, I'm staying, too."

"No, you need to get Cpl Dykstra under cover."

Cpl Mays shouted from across the street, "What are you two doing? Get moving!"

"Doc's staying. The lieutenant can't be moved, and neither can Zach," Rick called back.

"Doc, are you sure?" the squad leader asked.

"He's already made up his mind," Rick called back.

There was a pause, then Cpl Mays shouted out, "OK, we'll just have to cover you."

I was in a half kneeling position, keeping my head down, but still holding the lieutenant up. Rick was quiet for a moment before he reached over and hugged me. It was about as awkward a hug as could be, but it was most welcomed.

"Keep your head down, you stupid squid," he said quietly.

"You know it."

He got Cpl Dykstra in position, stood up, and vaulted across the open gap between the hummer and the wall. As with Jarod, he threw Dysktra over, then vaulted over himself. A machine gun opened up, throwing chips of plaster everywhere, but the gunner was too late. Rick was already over.

"You OK?" I asked though, just to be sure.

"Never fucking better," came his voice from the courtyard.

I looked around. I was alone with the lieutenant and two bodies, one Marine, and one Iraqi. For the first time since this started some five minutes ago, I could listen to what was going on. I could hear firing to the south and the sound of helos flying in support. I'd heard fiercer fighting before, but this was still a major operation.

There was a burst of fire every 30 seconds or so, more probably to keep our heads down than expecting to hit anything. I knew they'd have to bug out soon. They couldn't wait until our units arrived in force. Still, if that took too long, the lieutenant wouldn't make it.

I heard another crack from in back of me. Then, from in front, I heard the screaming of a man in pain. He cried out for about 20 seconds before falling silent. Looking back, I wondered who was the sniper team watching over me. Whoever the two guys were, they needed to keep their heads down. The machine guns started reaching up to the roofs, searching for them.

I was watching the rounds impact up there when a burst of rounds went off from my right. I felt like someone hit me on the head with a baseball bat. I spun around, whipping my M16 off my shoulder. Someone had crept up in the buildings closer to me and had me in his sights. I saw movement and fired three round bursts until my mag was empty.

From the other side of the road, the rest of the Marines must have seen where I was firing because they opened up as well, the SAWs putting up a lot of rounds and an M203 round actually flying in through a window. The grenade went off inside. Whether I had hit anyone, whether the squad had taken him out, or whether he had just bugged out, I didn't know. I just knew he had stopped firing at me.

The lieutenant started gurgling, and I lunged for him, putting him back up on his side. I reached up and felt my helmet. There was a crack right at the back. The round had not penetrated, though. My head hurt, but once again, I had to thank Sgt Butler, who had pretty much insisted I buy the BLSS helmet system before we left Lejeune. The system was not cheap, but I gave in, more for the comfort of the system over the standard issue helmet liner. Now, I was glad I had it. I probably would still have survived this shot with the issue liner, but I'd be hurtin' for certain much more, maybe down with a concussion.

I changed mags. I wished now that maybe I'd kept at least one more.

Over the next several minutes, I heard seven distinctive shots fired. I couldn't see the targets, but I hoped my guardian angel was taking his toll on the hajiis. If he was keeping them busy, they couldn't come after me.

"Still there, buddy?" Rick called out, his voice sounding like he was up a floor.

"Yep. Still here."

My head hurt and my finger was throbbing, but I was just happy to still be breathing. I couldn't see Pacman from where I was, and the lieutenant was struggling mightily to breathe, so I really couldn't complain.

Up ahead, maybe 50 meters, I heard the screeching of a gate open. This was on the right side of the street, the side with the bulk of the squad.

"Rick, something's happening!" I called out, disregarding the fact that anyone else could hear. The ragheads knew exactly where I was.

I heard a car gunning its engine, then it came out of a courtyard up ahead and turned towards me, hugging the walls. This kept them out of the line of fire from Cpl Mays and the rest of the squad, and they probably thought that it screened them from the sniper team. I lowered my M16 and empted my mag at them. I saw that I hit them, but they picked up speed and barreled down the wall. I didn't hear anything from above, so maybe they had figured out our sniper's position correctly. I was well and truly screwed.

I hopped over the lieutenant, putting my body between the car and him. There were three men in the car, all dressed in the black the insurgents preferred. One was driving while the other two held weapons at the ready. The driver caught my eye and smiled. He knew he had me.

One of the gunmen leaned out the window as he got a bead on me. He fired a burst that went over my head as the car bounced, not 20 meters away. A white flower suddenly blossomed in the windshield, and behind that flower, the driver jerked back. There was another crack, and the head of the gunman exploded into a pink mist. He fell, his body half in and half out of the car as it continued to move forward, drifting slightly to the right. Within an instant another round went out, taking out the second gunman.

The car slowed, but kept coming before plowing into the other hummer. The impact threw the dead gunman out of the car and up and over the hummer, his body sliding to a boneless stop not ten feet from me.

With a clear field of fire, the Marines and ISF opened up on the car, but that was overkill. In what had to be less than three seconds, three rounds had gone downrange and killed three insurgents. I looked back up and raised my hand to my helmet in a salute.

Firing like that evidently pinpointed his position, though, as all hell broke loose. The insurgents were hurt, but they had plenty of fight left in them. Automatic weapons focused on one specific rooftop. An RPG gunner stepped up from a building and kneeled, but he fell before he could fire. I wasn't sure how anyone could focus like that while under such an intense barrage. Another RPG went off, and almost in slow motion, I watched it rise until it impacted right at the edge of the roof with a huge explosion. When the smoke cleared, a chunk of the roof was simply gone, most likely the sniper team with it. The firing kept up for another minute, then died down.

An insurgent ran across the road 100 meters down. Nothing happened. No shots. Either they had taken out the team, or the team wanted to suck them in. I wanted the second of the two, but I feared the first.

I looked at my watch. It had only been about ten minutes since we got hit, even if it seemed like an hour. Surely the company would be charging to the rescue any minute now. I could hear copters in the air, but none flew over us.

I looked over to where I knew Rick was, but a flicker of movement in the adjacent building caught my eye instead. The bastards had been moving up.

"Rick! You've got company to your nine!" I shouted out.

I feverishly checked myself for another mag or a frag I might have somehow forgotten I had. Nothing.

The lieutenant, though, had a 9mm strapped to his thigh. It wasn't in one of the nylon military holsters, but in one of the commercial leg holsters, the hard plastic kind that most officers and SNCOs preferred. I reached over to take it, but the release had me confused. It would not let go of the Beretta.

I looked up just in time to see three black-clad hajiis rush out. I realized that just as the hummer had protected me from them earlier, now it protected them from the squad. But not from Rick. I heard a burst of fire, then another.

"You've got one on the other side of you, Zach!" Rick shouted. "I don't have a shot!"

I pulled at the 9mm, but it just wouldn't come free. I could actually hear heavy breathing on the other side of the hummer, not six feet away. If he came around, the rest of the squad couldn't fire for fear of hitting the lieutenant and me. I lay down across the lieutenant, pulling at the pistol. From this angle, I saw what looked to be a release button. I pressed it, and the pistol came free just as insurgent let out a shout and rushed around the front end of the hummer, AK lowered and firing. Only he hadn't lowered it enough, and the rounds went over my head. I raised the pistol, thumbing the safety, hoping that the lieutenant kept a round chambered.

I could see the shocked expression of the man as he saw me at his feet instead of crouching up higher. He started to swing his muzzle down as I pulled the trigger. Two rounds hit him in the chest, but either he got another shot off or his fingers spasmed as he died because a round caught me across my left shoulder.

I don't know what I expected. But he put two more rounds into the road beside me, straddling the lieutenant as he fell on top of us. For a moment, I thought he was attacking, and I struck out. But he was dead. I pushed him off the lieutenant, then looked at him. He had seemed so terrifying when all I heard was his breathing.

Now, he just looked small, so deflated. I felt a small rush of joy, but it was muted. I had just killed a man. I had fired my weapon before, and maybe I had hit someone. But I never knew if I had or hadn't. This time, there was no question. He was in front of me. I put two rounds into his chest. He was dead.

To be honest, I didn't feel much after that first flash of joy. He rushed us. I killed him. It was simple as that.

"Zach, Zach!" You OK?" Rick shouted out.

"Yea, we're still here. We're OK."

Then I looked at my shoulder. It hurt like a son-of-a-bitch, but even that, I almost noted as if it didn't matter. My emotions were numb. I reached up with my right hand and probed the shoulder. The round had gone right through the fleshy part of the shoulder, right above the triceps and just below the edge of the flak jacket. It didn't look like the bone had been hit.

Some of my blood had fallen on Lieutenant Hobbs. I reached over and tried to wipe it away. His breathing was getting shallower. If it stopped, I was going to start mouth-to-mouth through the flange end of the airway and not stop until a doctor pulled me off.

I didn't recognize the sound I'd been waiting for for a moment or two. But when the Cobra flashed over me, guns and rockets ablazing, well, I popped my head up to watch, shouting like an idiot. It made two passes before going off to help someone else.

A few minutes later, two hummers came up our back, guns ready. One stopped right beside me, and a Marine I vaguely recognized as a sergeant from Lima company jumped out.

"What d'ya got?" he asked.

"This is Lieutenant Hobbs, our platoon commander. He needs an emergency casevac. His airway is compromised," I told him.

"Doc, get over here," he shouted.

HM3 Charlie Wake jumped out of the second hummer and rushed over.

"He's barely hanging on," I told him. "He needs to get back now. His foot's trapped, though."

Charlie took over, getting Marines from Lima and my own Marines, who had come out, to physically lift the hummer up and over while I kept the lieutenant still. I was surprised, and more than a bit sad, to see Azar's crushed body from where the hummer had been. Charlie managed the move the lieutenant to one of the hummers. I wanted to stay with him, but Charlie told me I needed to stay with my squad, that he had the lieutenant now. We also got Jarod and Cpl Dykstra loaded, and the two hummers took off, their destination an impromptu LZ a couple hundred meters away.

I raised my arm, now bandaged courtesy of Charlie. I seemed to have full movement, even if it hurt to do so. I looked over to the courtyard where Pacman, Jerry, Azar, and the ISF soldier lay. I never even knew that jundii's name. We'd gotten orders to wait for SSgt White. Third squad had two wounded who needed a casevac, then a seven-ton was supposed to get us and bring us back. It looked like the fight was winding down.

Out in the road, we had pulled the six dead hajiis in a line and left them there. We could see at least one more down the road, but no one suggested we go down there to get him.

Of the three our sniper shot that were in the car, two had been hit in the face, one just where the neck met the chest. That was some amazing shooting.

"That was some shit, there, Zach," Rick said, coming up to me.

I was looking at the man I killed.

"Two shots, double tap!" he said.

"Nice shooting, Doc," Rob said, coming up behind me.

"Well, I couldn't very well miss. I mean, he was two feet from me."

"Shit, Doc, two feet? Couldn't you let him get a little closer?"

"Now, that, that's some shooting," I said, pointing to the three from the car.

"Yea, who did that? I couldn't see from where we were," Rob asked.

"Up there," I said, pointing to the ruined building in back of us. "We must have had a sniper team up there."

As I looked, I saw another flicker of movement. Was there someone in the building?

"Are they still there?" Rick asked.

"I don't know. They took a pretty big hit. Hey! Did you see that?" I asked.

I'd seen movement again, this time through ruined window on the second floor.

Everyone spun around, taking cover.

"What did you see, Doc?" Cpl Mays asked.

"Over there, where our snipers were. I'm sure there was movement."

"The snipers?" he asked me.

"I don't think so."

"What do we do," Cpl Dunlop asked.

"We've orders to stay here," the squad leader said, not sounding to adamant about it.

I knew Al Qaeda had a huge bounty on snipers. They hated them. And I remembered the sight of the two Marine snipers, heads cut off and placed on their chests. Dead or not, I did not want that to happen to anyone else, especially to two Marines who undoubtedly saved my ass.

"We've got to go," I said. "No one is going to mutilate two men who came to our call. They could've bugged out, but they kept the hajiis off our ass until the Cobra came."

Rick nodded and said, "Doc's right. And if not that, we need to secure this area. We can't wait and get on the truck only to have them hit us then."

Cpl Mays only hesitated a moment before nodding.

"Sounds righteous to me," he said.

"John, you stay here," he ordered.

Cpl Choi had dislocated his shoulder or clavicle breaking in the gate of the courtyard they'd retreated to.

"Rick and Noah, you're with me. We're taking, uh, La'Ron, Rob, and Cherrystone. Cy, you stay here with that SAW."

"I'm going, too," I said.

"Not to belabor the obvious, but you're messed up. You stay here," he replied.

"Sorry, that's not an option, corporal. You need me there, and if any sniper is by chance still alive, you'll need me."

The squad leader looked at Rick who simply shrugged.

"OK, you're in," he said. "Everyone locked and loaded?"

I'd taken Jerry's magazines, so I was ready. Cpl Mays went over our plan, such as it was. We were going in with seven of us, and we were going to move fast. We'd done this a million times, and we had to rely on our training.

We moved to the other side of the street, almost nonchalantly, as if we were just shifting our position. From there, we would be out of sight of our target, and we could scurry up to the building, hopefully unseen. With three corporals, we were a bit unbalanced in rank, so Rick took point.

The stack quickly moved up, using the buildings to screen us. We got up to our target. Rubble lay all around us, and the dust still in the air threatened to make me cough. I bit it back. We weren't going to be shouting out our movements. We wanted to get in, unseen and unheard.

Using hand and arm signals, Rick indicated he was going in left. Rob, right in back of him, was going in right. The rest of us would follow. Rick reached out and pushed open the door, which was barley hanging on by the hinges. I was afraid it would crash down, making a racket. He got the door open halfway, then slid inside. One by one, we were in.

It took a moment for our eyes to adjust to the dim light inside. This floor didn't look too damaged, but dust from the explosions above covered everything, clearly revealing several sets of footprints going up the stairs.

We started slowly going up the stairs. Halfway up the fist set, Rick held up his fist. We froze. We heard voices above us, subdued voices, but they were speaking Arabic. Rick took a few more steps up, then held up three fingers. Whoever it was, they were on the third floor.

It could be the home owners, checking the damage to the home now that the battle was almost over. It could be a couple of guys who wanted the reward for the snipers and would pick up the bodies, claiming the kill. Or it could be Al Qaeda foot soldiers.

We moved carefully up, our senses on full alert. There was more wall damage on this floor, so more light was coming in. We all gathered below the ladderwell to the next floor. Cpl Mays motioned to Rick and Cherrydick to check out the four rooms on this floor. We could hear movement above us, but that didn't mean there wasn't anyone on this floor as well.

Rick moved over to the first room, took a step inside before coming stepping back with a thumbs up. He motioned to the room across from him, and Cherrydick looked inside. He did a double take, then started to step in when Rick screamed out "No!"

He was lunging forward when the blast caught him.

The room had been booby trapped. I wanted to run over to him, but we had to move. Cpl Mays was shouting as we rushed up the stairs. There was shouting in Arabic, too, and shots rang out. Cpl Dunlop made it up the stairs first, firing as he ran. He went down at the top, but he didn't stop firing. We rushed past him. I was the third man up, and I was putting out three-round bursts. There were two insurgents in black at one end of the hall, and the three of us at the other end. All five of us stood there, weapons blazing. Somehow, no one was getting hit. I ran out of rounds and put in a new mag. It seemed like forever until at last, one of them took a round in the belly and folded over. His partner bolted to the side into the last room, a room that was fairly intact. It still had walls, at least.

I bolted after him, covering the short distance in seconds. Forgetting all my training, I simply burst into the room. In a flash, the two bloody Marines laying flat out on the deck and the insurgent lunging towards them with a huge machete-like knife registered like a photo. With my M16 at my hip, I fired another three-round burst, catching him in the side. He fell, dropping the knife.

He was alive, I could tell, but out of the fight. Rob came in right after me, and he kicked the knife out of the way.

I knelt beside the bloody bodies of the two Marines, checking to see if they'd been mutilated. And I recognized them. This was the team from the Government House, the odd-looking corporal and his tall a-gunner. Cpl Lindt.

He looked mostly intact. At least we had kept his remains from being desecrated. His family deserved that.

So I was completely surprised when Cpl Lindt opened his eyes, looked at me, and said, "Jeff's always getting after me to acknowledge others, so thank you."

Chapter 27

Hurricane Point
September 21, 2006

> *Amazing Grace, how sweet the sound,*
> *That saved a wretch like me.*
> *I once was lost but now am found,*
> *Was blind, but now I see.*

Those words ran through my head as the bagpipes wheezed to a halt. SSgt Kemper, the battalion's piper, had performed this service too many times over the last seven months. I looked around the chapel. It was standing room only, but that was the norm for memorial services.

In the front row, a number of stacks of pamphlets took up a couple of seats, one for each of the fallen. Beside them, the battalion commander and sergeant major, the company commander, the first sergeant, and the Army brigade commander from Camp Ramadi sat. In front of the chapel, beneath the pulpit, were photos of each man killed. These were men who were our brothers, men with whom we struggled and fought here in the desert thousands of miles from our homes.

The chaplain got up as the strains of the hymn faded away. He looked at us for several moments before he started talking, going on about righteousness, about sacrifice, about families and friends. To be honest, though, I wasn't really listening. I was thinking about those men we'd lost.

I didn't listen to the battalion CO, either. Oh, I heard his words while he praised each man, but they didn't register.

I looked back up at the photos in the front. At least the lieutenant's wasn't there. He was at Balad, waiting to go to Landstuhl and then back to Bethesda. He had a long road ahead of his as the doctors tried to reconstruct his jaw, but he was alive and out of danger. I was grateful for that.

Jarod was actually in worse shape. He was still in a coma with a severe Grade Three concussion. He was with the lieutenant at Balad ready for the long journey back.

Jonathan P. Brazee

The CO stepped down, and First Sergeant Thompson got up and stood in the front of the Chapel. He pulled out a paper, and cleared his throat.

"Acona, Marcus," he called out, his voice steady.

"Here," the lance corporal from First Platoon responded.

"Adams, Michael."

"Here, First Sergeant."

"Alderrama, Theobald," the company first sergeant continued.

"Here."

He slowly went down the list, naming each Marine and sailor in the company. He got through the A's and B's and into the C's.

"Cable, David."

"Here," Third Platoon's lieutenant called out, his voice strong and steady.

"Cannon, Derek."

"Here," I said quietly.

"Cherrystone, Lewis."

The chapel was quiet.

"Private First Class Lewis H. Cherrystone," the first sergeant said, his voice slightly louder.

Lewis? I thought. I was ashamed that I never even knew his first name.

The first sergeant waited a few more seconds before calling out a third and final time, "Private First Class Lewis H. Cherrystone."

Only silence greeted him.

"Private First Class Lewis Cherrystone, killed in action, September 19, 2006, Ramadi, Iraq," he intoned.

Three Marines, La'Ron one of them, marched forward, turning to face the photo of Cherrystone. La'Ron placed a rifle in the stand in front of the photo, then put a helmet on top of the rifle. Greg Marusky from his old platoon, the one that had essentially kicked him out, placed a pair of boots in front of the rifle, and Doug Miller, also from First, reached over and hung Cherrystone's dog tags from the M16. The three Marines stepped to the side.

"Chompers, Christian," the first sergeant continued his role call.

"Here, First Sergeant."

After four or five more names, he got to "Dykstra, Noah."

"Absent but accounted for," SSgt White responded.

This wasn't the only time we'd hear that during the ceremony. The lieutenant, Jarod, and four Marines from Second Platoon also had someone else speak up for them.

We made through the roles up into the H's.

148

"Haddad, Richard."

"Here, First Sergeant," Rick said in a weak voice.

I turned to look at my best friend. His face was torn up, both from shrapnel and from the flames, his arm was broken, and he had suffered a Grade 2 concussion, but nothing was going to keep him from attending the service. The brigade commander had picked him up at Charlie Medical and brought him over with him.

After Rick's name was called, I stared at Pacman's photo as the first sergeant made his way through the roll call. It wasn't as if we didn't know what was coming, but still I felt the tension build up until the first sergeant reached his name.

"Lopez, Emmanuel," he called out.

"Private First Class Emmanuel J. Lopez."

The chapel remained silent.

"Private First Class Emmanuel J. Lopez," rang out one last time.

The first sergeant waited a few moments, then went on. "Private First Class Emmanuel J. Lopez, killed in action, September 19, 2006, Ramadi, Iraq."

Rick, as Pacman's team leader, had wanted to place his M16 and helmet, but the doctors only let him come to the ceremony if he promised to sit through it, not participate in it. Cpl Mays, as the old fire team leader, Cpl Dunlop, who was limping from a minor leg wound, and Cy Pierce placed the rifle, helmet, boots, and dog tags in front of Pacman's photo. I struggled to hold back tears as they did so.

It took awhile to get through the next names, but I wished it would have taken longer. I know this is stupid, but I almost felt that if we didn't call out the names, then they weren't really gone yet. But inevitably, we got to Jerry.

"Scanlon, Gerald.

"Lance Corporal Gerald G. Scanlon.

"Lance Corporal Gerald G. Scanlon."

There was no reply.

"Lance Corporal Gerald G. Scanlon, killed in action, September 19, 2006, Ramadi, Iraq."

Cpl Choi, his arm in a sling, Rob Runolfson, and Frank Gandy, a hometown friend of Jerry's from H & S Company placed his items.

There was only one photo left. I got myself ready.

It was only a few moments more until the first sergeant called out, "Seychik, Buster."

Buster had been killed trying to save one of the ISF soldiers with his squad. The soldier had been hit in the back and was in the

---

middle of the road, screaming in pain. Buster knew that the insurgents were waiting for someone to rush to the man's aid, but he couldn't let him suffer. He rushed out, grabbed the man by his harness, and started to drag him to safety when a burst of machine gun fire caught him. The guys in his squad said that even wounded, he still tried to drag the ISF soldier out of the line of fire when another burst killed him and the soldier both.

"Hospital Corpsman Third Class Buster B. R. Seychik."

Then one last time, "Hospital Corpsman Third Class Buster B. R. Seychik."

As the first sergeant said, "Hospital Corpsman Third Class Buster B. R. Seychik, killed in action, September 19, 2006, Ramadi, Iraq" I stepped out with the other two Marines.

I had been surprised when SSgt Smith had told me that Buster had said that if anything ever happened to him, he wanted me to be one of his attendants at the memorial. I followed Sgt Smith and Cpl Stanborough out. The squad leader placed the rifle and helmet, Cpl Stanborough the boots. Once they were done, I placed Buster's dog tags over the butt of the M16.

I got along with Buster well enough, but I really had thought him to be too gung ho, too officious. He wasn't "my kind of guy." Now I felt guilty for that. I'm not sure what he'd seen in me to warrant this honor.

I burst into tears as we made our right face and marched off. The tears weren't just for Buster. They were for all of them. For Steve Potts. For Sgt Butler. For Pacman, Jarod, Steve Jenner. For Azar. These were tears for my brothers.

The rest of the ceremony consisted of Marines and sailors standing up and saying a few words about each of the fallen. I didn't listen. I already knew the temper of their steel. I didn't need anyone else to try and tell more.

After the 21-gun salute, I went to get ready for the night's patrol. We still had a war to fight.

Epilogue

Camp Lejeune, North Carolina
November 21, 2006

"There's my boy," I said, taking Tyson from Amy's arms.

I held him out from me for a moment, reading the writing on his green t-shirt. Amy had got it done out in town, making a mini-copy of the shirt the squad had given me when we got back.

THE MARINES HAVE ALREADY FOUND THEIR FEW GOOD MEN

U.S. NAVY CORPSMEN

"Hah, that looks great," I told her as I gave her a kiss.

I had been jealous of the other guys whose wives met us as we landed at Cherry Point last month. Amy and I had decided that we just couldn't afford the ticket, especially as I was going back to California during my post-deployment leave. I enjoyed my leave in El Cajon, bonding with Tyson and getting reacquainted with my wife. Parting again so soon was a blow, and a week after I got back to the battalion, we decided enough was enough. We scraped together enough for her and Tyson to follow me to Lejeune. We were staying with Jason Dougherty, a corpsman from India Company, taking a small room in their trailer. It was small and cramped, but Amy thought it was oddly romantic being "trailer trash."

Carol, Jason's wife, thought it was great having a baby around, passing hints to Jason that maybe it was time for them to start their own family, but it had only been a few days, and I knew having guests could get old pretty quick. I hoped base housing would open up soon. Even as a newly promoted IIN, the VHA for an E3 wouldn't cover the rent for an apartment in J-ville.

"So this is the little Doc Cannon?" SSgt White said, coming over. He looked at Amy. "And you are the lovely Mrs. Cannon, I presume. I feel I know you already," he said, taking her hand delicately. "Zach here could not keep quiet about you, and now that I see you, I can understand why."

I looked at the acting platoon commander in awe. He had completed four complete sentences without once dropping the F-bomb. Who was this and what had they done with the real SSgt White?

The four of us walked into the company office. Cpl Morrison jumped up and offered Amy a seat on the couch, asking if she needed anything. She declined, but I could see in the glow in her eyes that she appreciated the attention. She'd been a "Navy Wife" for more than a year, but she really hadn't been around the military, other than going to PX at 32nd Street or Balboa to give birth.

Gunny Tora came in and made his introductions, then the XO. The first sergeant came out of his office and asked me if I knew what I was supposed to do. We'd gone over it about a million times already, so I assured him I was ready.

At about 1245, Captain Wilcox returned from wherever he'd been, probably either PT or chow. He shook Amy's hand, telling her how proud the company was of me. I knew it was all BS for Amy's sake, but still, hearing the commander say that felt rather good. He invited us into his office where we sat and chatted. I should say the captain and Amy chatted. I didn't know what to say. This was my company commander, and I didn't have a habit of just chatting up Marine captains. Amy, though, was in her element. She was never at a loss for words, and I was happy to let her take over.

The first sergeant interrupted us, sticking his head in the office and telling the captain that is was time. We got up and went outside to the parking lot where we held formations. The company was already in formation, waiting for us.

Cpl Morrison came up, offered his arm to Amy, and escorted her to a chair that had been placed to the front and off to the side of the formation. He then took position to her side and went to parade rest. Most of the battalion corpsmen were alongside her as well, including the senior chief. Even the chaplain was there as the senior Navy member of the battalion. I did not accompany her but went to take my place in the back of the formation.

The first sergeant called the company to attention, went through his formalities, and made an about face to turn the company over to the skipper. As Captain Wilcox marched forward, the three officer platoon commanders took their place in front of their platoons. I wished Lieutenant Hobbs could have been there, but he was still up at Bethesda. He had sent me a nice letter, though, giving his regrets.

The first sergeant stepped to the side of the company commander and called out, "Personnel to be recognized, front and center . . .march!"

I made a right face and started marching, going along the back and then up alongside the headquarters element before making another left turn to march along the front of the formation up to the captain. I halted, did a right face, and saluted. He returned the salute, and I came back to attention. I felt dizzy, and I prayed I wouldn't pass out.

The first sergeant's voice, toned by two tours on the drill field, boomed out:

DEPARTMENT OF THE NAVY

THIS   IS   TO   CERTIFY   THAT
THE SECRETARY OF THE NAVY HAS AWARDED THE

NAVY AND MARINE CORPS ACHIEVEMENT MEDAL

WITH COMBAT DISTINGUISHING DEVICE

TO

HOSPITALMAN ZACHARY L. CANNON, UNITED STATES NAVY

FOR HEROIC ACHIEVEMENT IN CONNECTION WITH COMBAT OPERATIONS AGAINST THE ENEMY WHILE SERVING AS A CORPSMAN WITH KILO COMPANY, THIRD BATTALION, EIGHT MARINES ON JULY 26, 2006.   WHILE CONDUCTING OPERATIONS AGAINST A CONCERTED ENEMY ATTACK, FIRST SQUAD, SECOND PLATOON WAS SPLIT FROM THE REMAINDER OF THE PLATOON BY HEAVY AUTOMATIC WEAPONS FIRE. WHEN A MARINE BECAME A CASUALTY IN NEED OF IMMEDIATE CARE, THEN HOSPITALMAN APPRENCTICE CANNON VOUNTEERED TO BRAVE THE WITHERING FIRE TO GO TO THE MARINE'S AID. WITH DISREGARD TO HIS OWN SAFETY, HE CROSSED THE ENEMY KILL ZONE, REACHING THE SQUAD'S POSITION WHERE HE RENDERED LIFESAVING MEDICAL TREATMENT.   HN CANNON'S PROFESSIONALISM WHILE UNDER FIRE AND HIS CONCERN FOR HIS FELLOW MARINES OVER HIS OWN PERSONAL SAFETY REFLECT GREAT CREDIT UPON HIMSELF,

Jonathan P. Brazee

AND WERE IN KEEPING WITH THE HIGHEST TRADITIONS OF
THE US NAVY AND THE U.S. NAVAL SERVICE.
G. H. HARRISON

LIEUTENANT COLONEL, COMMANDING

As the first sergeant finished, the company commander
reached forward to pin the medal to the pocket flap of my cammies.
He stepped back, then shook my hand. I started to salute out of
habit, but caught myself and came back to attention.

As with my Army Achievement Medal, I was somewhat
ambivalent about this one. It might have been different if Sgt
Castanza had made it, but with him passing, I hardly felt my efforts
really mattered much.

The first sergeant cleared his throat and started reading again:

THE UNITED STATES NAVY
THIS IS TO CERTIFY THAT THE NAVY ENLISTED
FLEET MARINE FORCE WARFARE SPECIALIST BADGE

HAS BEEN AWARDED TO
HOSPITALMAN ZACHARY L. CANNON
FOR SUCCESSFULT COMPLETION OF THE COURSE
MATERIAL AS PRESCRIBED BY THE SECRETARY OF THE
NAVY
GIVEN ON THIS 20TH DAY OF NOVEMEBER, 2006

THOMAS R. HADDERATY
MAJOR GENERAL, COMMANDING

As the skipper reached over to pin the badge above my pocket,
I felt a surge of pride. This really meant more to me than any medal.
This was acceptance. I hadn't planned on getting qualified. It
wasn't going to do me much good in a hospital, but thinking back on
the Marines I served with, and thinking on Buster Seychik, well, it
just made sense. It was awarded to me, but it was also a tribute to
them. This was my salute to those we'd lost.

It hadn't been that difficult, to be honest. I was given credit
for much of what I'd done in Iraq. I'd gone out one day with an MP
company to fam fire some weapons, which I would have jumped at
the chance to do anyway. The M19, in particular, was a trip to fire. I
had to take some tests on general knowledge. The worst thing was
getting grilled by the command master chief, our battalion senior

chief, and another senior chief. I had been pretty nervous standing before those three, but I made it through. And now I had my FMFEWS. It was something that I would cherish for the rest of my life.

I'd been told that I'd been put in for a pretty high award for the action where Pacman, Jarod, and Cherrystone had died. Whatever came of that, I think this simple badge would mean more. I joined the Navy for technical training, but I had built up a sense of pride in the Navy and in my service to it. This badge showed me that the Marine Corps valued me, too.

This time, I did salute the skipper, did a left face, then marched to the rear of the formation. The skipper turned it over to the first sergeant who then dismissed us. I wanted to go right to Amy, but I had to get through a pretty big group of well-wishers. My back felt bruised from all the pounding it took.

I finally got to Amy. She reached out to touch the Achievement Medal. The bright green with orange stripes and the bright gold V in the middle looked more impressive to her then the silver-colored badge. Tyson liked it, too. When he leaned forward to let him see, he grabbed it and tried to put it in his mouth.

I had the rest of the day off, but the squad was taking Amy and me to the Harvey House, all the way in New Bern, so we planned to stick around on base. I'd never been there, but Cpl Mays assured me it was pretty high class.

"I'm afraid I need to steal your husband, here, Mrs. Cannon," senior chief finally said. "I'll have him back to you in a few minutes."

I looked at Amy, raising my eyebrows in an unspoken question. She looked deep into my eyes, then nodded. Good, nothing had changed, then. I turned and followed the senior chief to the battalion aid station and into his office. He sat down behind his desk, indicating with his hand for me to take a seat as well.

"You done good there, Zach. You've made the Navy proud."

I didn't say anything.

"You made the right decision on earning your badge. I just ask you to wear it with pride at your next duty station. You may be in a hospital, but show that world that you succeeded as a corpsman with the Marines."

"Aye-aye Senior Chief. Don't worry, I'll wear it."

"Well, we're going to hate to lose you, but me and the sergeant major got the CO, and he got the regimental CO to push it."

He opened a folder and took out a set of orders, sliding them across the desk at me.

"You've earned it." he said.

I looked at them. They were orders to C-School to earn my HM-8407 enlisted code, the code given to radiation health technicians. From there, I was going to Naval Hospital Bethesda.

"Well?" he asked when I didn't say anything.

I flicked the missing tip of my little finger with my thumb, a habit I'd picked up when I felt stressed. I hesitated, then plunged forward.

"Sorry, Senior Chief, I can't accept these," I managed to get out.

"What? What do you mean? Do you know how lucky you are? Do you know how many people went up to bat for you? I know you wanted Balboa, but billets are billets, and three purple hearts and whatever else you're getting or not, it's still needs of the service," he sputtered.

I could see he was surprised and not too happy about what I'd said.

"And I appreciate that, Senior Chief, I really do. But Amy and I've been talking seriously about my future, about our future. I'm only 20 years old, and I've got a wife and son. I've got to do what's right for them, and as Amy tells me, I've got to do what's right for me. I need to be happy in my job."

"What? You don't mean you want an early out, do you? If you do, that's not going to happen."

"What?" I parroted, not understanding.

"What do you mean, 'what?' Are you trying to get out of your service commitment?"

"Uh, no, Senior Chief, why do you ask me that?"

"Well then what the fuck are you getting at?"

I looked down at the silver badge on my breast before answering.

"I'm a Fleet Marine Force corpsman now, Senior Chief. This is where I belong. I've found my home, and this is where I need to stay."

Other Books by Jonathan Brazee

The Return of the Marines Trilogy

The Few
The Proud
The Marines

The Al Anbar Chronicles: First Marine Expeditionary Force—Iraq

Prisoner of Fallujah
Combat Corpsman
Sniper (working title)

To The Shores of Tripoli

Darwin's Quest: The Search for the Ultimate Survivor

Wererat

Author Website

http://www.returnofthemarines.com

Glossary

A School	The initial school after boot camp where sailors learn a skill
Al Qaeda	Short for Al Qaeda in Iraq, mostly made up of foreign fighters
C School	A follow-on school for advanced training
CASEVAC	Casualty Evacuation
Corps School	Common name for the hospitalman A school
Cpl	Corporal
DFAC	Dining Facility
EPW	Enemy Prisoner of War
Fobbit	A person who never goes out beyond the wire, one who stays at the Forward Operating Base
HA	Hospitalman Apprentice, an E2
Hajii	Slang for Iraqi or Arab
IED	Improvised Explosive Device
ITT	Interrogation/Interrogator Translator Team
Jundii	Slang for an Iraqi ISF soldier
LCpl	Lance Corporal
MCMAP	Marine Corps Martial Arts Program
MIA	Missing in Action
MiTT	Military Transition Team
MNF	Multi-National Force
O6	Designator for the rank of colonel
PRT	Provincial Reconstruction Team
PTT	Police Transition Teams
RPG	Rocket-Propelled Grenade
SNCO	Staff Non-Commissioned Officer
STA	Surveillance and Target Acquisition Platoon
T/O	Table of Organization
USAID	United States Agency for International Development

Made in the USA
San Bernardino, CA
24 April 2018